A Candlelight Ecstasy Romance®

"MR. WHEELER—"

"John," he prompted.

"Okay . . . John." Rebecca adopted her best school-marmish voice to counteract the effect of his magnetic pull. He had a certain charm that was difficult to resist. "We're two strangers brought together for business purposes. Because we don't know each other we can expect to have—misunderstandings. We must establish the trust necessary between a teacher and a pupil, be forthright with each other."

"Okay, I'll buy that."

"Good," she said, smiling. But deep down, she knew she was breaking her own rule. Because as much as she tried to hide it, she was attracted to him, and right now, a business relationship was not all she had on her mind. . . .

CANDLELIGHT ECSTASY CLASSIC ROMANCES

DENIM AND SILK

Anna Hudson

A CANDLELIGHT ECSTASY ROMANCE®

Published by
Dell Publishing Co., Inc.
1 Dag Hammarskjold Plaza
New York, New York 10017

Dell ® TM 681510, Dell Publishing Co., Inc.

Candlelight Ecstasy Romance®, 1,203,540, is a registered
trademark of Dell Publishing Co., Inc., New York, New York.

ISBN: 0-440-11853-0

Printed in the United States of America

September 1987

10 9 8 7 6 5 4 3 2 1

KRI

To Our Readers:

As of September 1987, Candlelight Romances will cease publication of Candlelight Ecstasies and Supremes. The editors of Candlelight would like to thank our readers for 20 years of loyalty and support. Providing quality romances has been a wonderful experience for us and one we will cherish. Again, from everyone at Candlelight, thank you!

Sincerely,

The Editors

DENIM AND SILK

CHAPTER ONE

"Big as a grizzly bear and equally ornery," Diana Feldman groaned as she passed Rebecca Sterling a black and white snapshot. "Without your help, he's utterly hopeless, a throwback from the mail-order-bride generation. Can you believe that *this* wants a 'lady'?"

Rebecca watched Diana roll her eyes heavenward as though beseeching a higher being for guidance. Plucking the picture from her ex-roommate's manicured fingers, she started to say, "He can't be that bad," but changed her mind. John Wheeler fit Diana's description. A mountain of a man, she thought, judging his size from the massive boulder in the background of the picture. But his height wouldn't be a problem. The female clients of Diana's matchmaking service would appreciate his thoroughly male physique. Unfortunately, his face was barely discernible behind his dark, full beard and shaggy eyebrows. Diana's clients expected to be fixed up with a suave, debonair executive, not the first cousin of the Indomitable Snowman.

"Do yourself a favor. Send him a refund. It's going to take more than a crash course in civilized behavior to change him into a refined gentleman. Your clients expect their dates to arrive at their door with a bouquet of long-stemmed red roses. From the looks of the man in this picture, he'd probably be munching on them."

Diana tapped her lower lip with her forefinger thoughtfully. "You wouldn't say that if you saw the postdated bonus check he included with his picture and financial statement."

"Rich?" Rebecca asked as she noted the worn flannel shirt and jeans on the man in the picture. A derelict in downtown Denver wouldn't be envious of Mr. Wheeler's clothing.

"Mmm. Fabulously. I ran a profile on him. The man is practically a legend in Montana. He's got the Midas touch with a twentieth-century twist. Every rock he picks up doesn't turn into gold . . . it turns into precious stones. He found a star sapphire that qualifies for the *Guinness Book of World Records*."

Intrigued, Rebecca leaned forward in the plush leather chair, nodding her head as she placed his name. "Wheeler? Is this J. C. Wheeler? Montana's mystery man?"

"You've heard of him?"

"Anyone in the jewelry business has read about

J. C. Wheeler. Granted, I specialize in goldsmithing, but he's been written up in several trade journals. Everyone from rockhounds to reporters have tried to locate his hidey-hole."

She studied the picture more closely. Although his eyes were partially hidden beneath a lock of wind-blown hair, there was something undefinable about them that mesmerized her. Black eyes, she thought. Black as onyx. Recalling the conflicting rock folklore she studied, she wondered if J. C. Wheeler's eyes would cool the ardor of love in the same way that wearing the stone around the neck was supposed to do, or would his black eyes protect against all evil?

"I guess that explains his reluctance to stay in Denver while he's groomed." Diana grinned when she saw Rebecca shake her head. "No? In all the old western movies gold miners were always having their claims jumped while the miners were in the big city celebrating. Doesn't that still happen?"

"Not to my knowledge. From what I've read, Wheeler is a hermit. He hasn't registered his claim because he doesn't want anybody poking around in his territory." She glanced at the picture for another look at his enigmatic face. "What I don't understand is why he's come to you looking for a wife. I'd think there would be plenty of local women who'd sell their souls to become Mrs. J. C. Wheeler."

11

Diana unfolded two sheets of lined notebook paper and read aloud, "I want a *real lady*. No gold-diggers, please." She passed the first page of the letter to Rebecca. "He must have had some unsavory women chasing him. Frankly, the old platitude about marrying for money and earning it the rest of your life should be the caption beneath his picture."

"He certainly has old-fashioned ideas about what a lady is, doesn't he?" Rebecca said, chuckling as she read his itemized list.

"I'll say. When I read it, I started looking through my files for a women who wears starched petticoats, a corset, and a sun bonnet. That's when I thought of you," Diana blurted.

Rebecca raised one blond eyebrow. During their college days, Diana had teased her unmercifully about her collection of pristine white cotton underwear. Remembering the buttercup-yellow scraps of silk she presently wore brought a secretive smile to her lips.

Twenty-six, she mused, was eons away from being eighteen and under her mother's restrictive eagle eyes. Once she'd become financially independent from her parents, she'd gone on a clothing binge that would have shocked Diana. Now the hope chest her mother had given her overflowed with silk and satin lingerie. Her closets were filled with soft, sensuous clothing that whispered against her skin. Oh yes, she'd kept a set of cotton underwear as a reminder, but she hadn't worn it in years.

Her blue eyes dropped back to the picture she still held in her hand. "I hope your matchmaking schemes don't include me."

"Of course not," Diana disclaimed a bit too abruptly and loudly for Rebecca's comfort.

Rebecca rose to her feet, shaking her head. Her silver-blonde hair swung across her slender shoulders.

"Okay. I admit it. At first I did sort of play with the idea of fixing you up with John." Diana shrugged as though she'd casually dismissed the idea.

"You know I'm not interested in getting married. It took me five years to get out from under my parents' benign dictatorship. I'm not about to let some mountain man take over where they left off. I'm perfectly happy with my life, thank you very kindly."

"I said I toyed with the idea." Her eyes traveled from Rebecca's chic hair style down the front of her silk shirtwaist dress. "Five years ago, you'd have been perfect. Unfortunately for John Wheeler, you've changed. Gold and precious gems belong together, but a city girl and a hermit? A liberated woman and a mountain man? No, I pride myself on making good, solid matches. I contacted you for exactly the reasons I gave you. He needs somebody to spiffy him up

13

before he arrives in Denver. With the right clothes and decent manners, I won't have any problems finding him a suitable 'lady.' "

Diana is hiding something, Rebecca ascertained as she watched her friend's eyes dart around the office. Knowing Diana couldn't tell a fib without giving herself away by being extremely nervous, Rebecca dropped the letter and picture on the top of the desk. "And?"

"And what?" Diana crossed her arms over her chest defensively.

"Come on, Diana. You're up to something other than matchmaking. We're friends. What is it?"

"N-n-nothing that concerns our friendship," came Diana's stammered response. "You've done consultant work before."

"Locally," Rebecca injected, disliking the idea of bundling up the necessary paraphernalia to do the job properly: a set of dishes, silverware, crystal, clothing.

"I thought I could count on you."

"Don't lay a guilt trip on me. My mother has exclusive rights to that ploy. She has it down to a fine art." Exasperated by her friend's unwillingness to confide in her, she said, "Do you honestly expect me to blithely trek out to the wilds of Montana to civilize a mountain man so you can find him a mate, without knowing why it's so important to you?"

14

"While you were building your reputation in the jewelry business, I helped you by letting you do consultant work for my agency. Since when have you become so suspicious of my motives?"

"Since you haven't been able to look me in the eye." Rebecca splayed her fingertips and leaned on the desk, her pose demanding a straight answer. "What's the problem?"

Diana appeared to crumple right before Rebecca's eyes. Her shoulders slumped; she lifted her hands, then covered her eyes. "Money."

"Money?" Rebecca repeated, astounded by Diana's admission.

The Sterlings were paupers compared to the Feldmans. All Diana had to do to was snap her fingers and her father's chauffeur would hand-deliver a check for any amount Diana needed. Silently she groaned as she remembered the current battle being waged between Diana and her father. Mr. Feldman had insisted that his daughter stop her "silly matchmaking business" and get married. He even pushed the point by slyly introducing her to several young executives at family social functions. Rebecca knew Diana would have to swallow her pride if she went to her parents for help.

"I made some bad financial investments. Nothing drastic. As long as I keep my cash flow going for another two or three months, I'll be okay.

Wheeler's bonus check would make a big difference," Diana explained.

"How much do you need?"

She gave a low whistle when she heard Diana's answer, then said, "You're welcome to the money in my savings account, but . . ."

"Thanks, but no thanks. You wouldn't take money from me when you needed it. I'm not going to take money from you, either. What I need is a big favor."

Rebecca understood Diana's refusal, but she was still hesitant to traipse off to Montana. "Why don't *you* go to Montana? We graduated from the same finishing school. You know as much as I do about proper social behavior."

"I can't go anywhere. I have to keep the business running smoothly or I'll be in worse trouble." Diana stood up and crossed the window. "You know, I think the real reason I called you was for inspiration. Each time I've considered bagging it in and saying to hell with making it on my own, I'll let some man take care of me, I think of you. You don't let anyone fight your battles for you."

Slightly embarrassed by her friend's compliments, Rebecca said, "Don't let my gold bracelets confuse you. They don't protect me from life's little bullets. I'm not Wonder Woman."

Diana chuckled. "Aren't you? I swear, if the world's gold mines ran dry, you'd be out there with a pick and shovel determined to find a new mother lode."

"And if I needed help carting the sack of gold down the mountainside, you'd be there." Rebecca sighed, knowing she couldn't refuse to help her friend. She moved to Diana's side and looped her arm across her distraught friend's shoulders and gave her a warm smile. "Wheeler's post-dated check is your mother lode. Guess you'd better find me a king-sized gunny sack to cart him back to Denver in."

Diana hugged Rebecca. "I knew I could count on you." Not allowing time for Rebecca to change her mind, she added, "Can you leave for Montana tomorrow?"

"I . . ." Rebecca disliked being rushed into anything. Mentally she went over her schedule. There wasn't any project that demanded immediate attention—she'd just completed an enameled brooch that had been accepted on consignment by Denver's most reputable jewelry dealer—and postponing her departure would be like putting a vise on Diana's cash flow. Her friend needed help . . . now. "Where do I go and how do I get there?"

"You're to fly into Billings." She scurried to her desk and picked up the second page of the letter. "I'll arrange the flight. Thank God for charge cards," she muttered under her breath.

Suddenly curious as to the exact whereabouts

17

of the reclusive J. C. Wheeler, Rebecca asked, "Billings? The Yogo Sapphire Mines are close to Garneill. That's north of Billings."

"Well, uh," Diana folded and refolded the piece of paper until it was small enough to pop into her mouth and swallow. "You won't be going north from what he's said in his letter."

"Look, Diana, I'm willing to go the extra mile in the name of friendship, but I'm not going to take one step out of Denver without knowing exactly what my destination is." A mental picture of Wheeler's black eyes reminded her that the onyx was also responsible for discord between friends. Was she overreacting? Did it really matter where she tutored Diana's client?

She raised her hands before Diana could respond. "Never mind. I'll have to respect his privacy, I suppose."

"To be honest with you, Mr. Wheeler didn't say exactly where you'd be taken. All the letter says is that if you needed to be contacted for an emergency, you could be reached through a general delivery post office box in Sacrifice Cliff." Laughing a bit shrilly, she added, "I was intrigued by the name, so I looked it up. It's where Crow braves threw themselves to their deaths hoping to appease the Great Spirit during a smallpox epidemic."

"I hope that isn't prophetic of this trip into the wilds of Montana," Rebecca commented as she picked up her purse. "I have a sneaky feeling I may want to hurl myself off a cliff before this assignment is completed."

"There is one other little thing Mr. Wheeler requested," Diana said with a weak smile as she reached into her top desk drawer. She extracted a piece of cloth. "I'm to make certain you take a blindfold."

Laughing at such an absurd attempt to keep his location a secret, she scoffed, "Do I have to promise not to peek?"

"No, but I did have to send him a notarized letter giving my word of honor you wouldn't reveal where you're going or afterward, where you've been. I guess he's protecting himself from the media."

Rebecca tossed back her head and laughed harder. "He isn't leaving anything to chance, is he?"

"Nothing. He seems to be a man who knows exactly what he wants and goes after it—no holds barred."

Later that evening after Rebecca had packed her suitcases, those words echoed in her mind as she read a feature article in a back issue of *Rockfinders* magazine.

According to the article, J.C. was the son of a prospector who roamed the mountains futilely searching for gold. There was no mention of his mother.

"Sounds like a lousy childhood," Rebecca muttered aloud, flipping the page and searching for a photograph. A child being moved from pillar to post, while the father meandered from one isolated area to another, wasn't her idea of how to properly raise a young boy. More than likely he was poorly educated and had few friends, if any.

Friendship and loyalty were important to Rebecca. She could count the number of close friends she had on one hand. But, it was a comfort to know they were there if she needed them —or, in Diana's case, if they needed her. Wheeler could count his friends with a closed fist, she mused, feeling somewhat sorry for the poor man.

Poor man? Materialistically speaking, he's one of the richest men in Montana from all accounts, she corrected. He can buy anything he wants. Knowing she was the kind of woman who always favored the underdog, Rebecca tried to keep J. C. Wheeler's situation in the proper perspective. Just because *she* would be unhappy living the lifestyle of a hermit didn't mean he would.

Deliberately she veered her concentration back to the article. Brilliant displays of gemstones being held by a pair of masculine hands added vibrant colors to the slick pages. Much to her dismay, she found herself searching for Wheeler's photograph. A one-line phrase that captioned the final picture explained the reason: "Personal photograph unavailable."

As she closed the magazine, a mental image of black eyes and tousled hair flashed in her mind. His eyes appealed to her. There seemed to be something in them silently beckoning her.

"That's ridiculous," she muttered disparagingly. "He had the picture taken for Diana to see, not me."

She tossed the magazine on the glass-topped table. She had to keep her reason for going to Montana clearly focused in her mind. Wheeler was the kind of man who knew what he wanted and obtained it. Presently, he wanted a wife, a *lady* wife. Before he could meet his objective, he had to give the appearance of being a gentleman. Thanks to her friend's precarious financial position, that was her job. Period. She wouldn't allow her generous nature to make assumptions that might or might not be true.

"Wheeler isn't a stray cat looking for a warm bed and a bowl of ice cream," she stated firmly.

Wondering about Wheeler's background, being stymied by lack of information, and being certain she was jumping to all the wrong conclusions about the mysterious man, her thoughts delved into introspection.

Rebecca knew who she was and where she'd come from. Although she'd been born with the proverbial silver spoon in her mouth, her child-

hood hadn't been easy, either. Isolation and loneliness weren't always caused by living in a remote
location.

Rising from the tan leather sofa, she crossed
the living room to the glass cabinet displaying
several enameled gold works of art she'd de-
signed, made to sell, and then been unable to part
with. Careful not to jar the glass shelves, she
opened the cabinet.

From habit, she chose the first gold enameled
brooch she'd made. She critically examined it. By
her present standards, it was somewhat crude.

She'd always been fascinated by gold and silver
jewelry, even as a child. By all rights, she probably should have hated it, since her mother considered her jewelry box of far more value than her
rambunctious child. On second thought, Rebecca
realized it was natural for her to appreciate quality craftsmanship. Her mother had only the best.

During her teenage years, Rebecca discounted
the glitzy appeal of the precious stones that her
mother preferred and became fascinated with the
workmanship of the metal. The setting, rather
than the stone, became the focus of her attention.
And yet, she loved vibrant colors.

Rebecca rubbed her thumb over the raised texture of the brooch. Enameling, the combination
of glass-making and metallurgy—two of the old-
est crafts known to man—was a natural for her.
It combined working with precious metals and

adding color. The translucent blue background of the brooch gave the illusion of a summer sky. In the center, a golden eagle appeared to be soaring through it.

The completion of this piece of jewelry was significant. It heralded her independence from family ties. Her parents had objected to her "piddling around" in the jewelry business. Clare, her mother, considered Rebecca's early efforts at goldsmithing as merely "artsy, teenage rebellion." Her father, Howard, wasn't home enough to be bothered with a daughter who couldn't be groomed to take over the family business. But eventually, Clare nagged Howard long enough to get her daughter out of her hair, too. They'd sent her to a finishing school in Switzerland to get rid of her "silly ideas" about becoming an artist.

Within the first few months of being abroad, Rebecca learned several lessons. Punishment for unladylike behavior was swift. A recalcitrant pupil was closeted in her room to think about her misdeeds. Already banished from her home, Rebecca intensely disliked being isolated from her new-found friends. Quickly, she learned the rules and gave the appearance of abiding by them.

She was rebellious, but not stupid.

By biting her tongue she could restrain her hot temper. A vacuous smile replaced the unacceptable lopsided curling of her lip. She sugar-coated her blunt opinions until they sounded as sweet and pure as the chapel's bells.

Her academic course-work in music, literature, and art appreciation were a breeze. She excelled, especially in the latter, much to Clare's dislike. After all, her daughter's interest in art was supposed to be minimized.

But most important, Rebecca gained self-confidence. Just because her mother considered her a constant bother did not mean she was worthless. Her peers found her friendly, loyal, and outrageously funny. She kept them in stitches with her good-natured imitations of the instructors.

She returned to Denver solid as gold. Like the delicate hues of an enameled piece of artwork, she blended all she'd learned without losing her true colors. She was her own woman.

Fortunately for Rebecca, by the time she'd graduated, returned home, and completed her early pieces of jewelry, enameled jewelry had become popular. Within weeks of completing the brooch, she had several other pieces completed and sold them on consignment for a relatively small amount of money. She moved out of her spacious room in her parent's mansion to a tiny apartment.

Diana had helped her gain financial independence by paying a consultant fee for tutoring prospective clients. As the quality of her work improved with practice, the amount of money

Rebecca earned increased. She did less and less consultant work, and spent more and more time honing her craft.

She wasn't rich. According to her parent's standards, she was one step above the poverty level. But she was secure. Money wasn't how Rebecca measured success. She had her home, her friends, and her work.

"What more could I ask for?" she whispered as she placed the brooch back on the shelf and closed the cabinet. She noticed a slight tremor of her fingers. The question left her feeling unsettled.

She'd told Diana she was happy. She'd meant it, hadn't she? Of course, she had, she reassured herself. Then why the jitters? A brief trip to Montana to tame a mountain man certainly wouldn't change anything.

Scoffing at the trepidation she was experiencing, she attributed it to the secrecy surrounding her destination. It was perfectly normal to be a bit frightened of the unknown. Rebecca groaned aloud. J. C. Wheeler could definitely be classified as an "unknown" too.

Determined to stay on top of the situation, she mentally examined the information she did have. Air travel didn't bother her. She enjoyed it. Billings, Montana, was a thriving metropolitan area. No reason for being afraid. She'd seen Wheeler's picture. Recognizing him at the airport wouldn't be difficult. All she had to do was watch for the first pre-Neanderthal man walking by and grab him.

Her innate sense of humor and vivid imagination made her chuckle at the mental picture rather than cringe.

I'll cope. I'll do better than cope. J. C. Wheeler, you're going to change into a dapper gentleman in record-breaking time.

Briskly striding into her bedroom, she removed her cosmetic case from the edge of the bed, turned back the sheets, and climbed in. Her positive attitude and her pep talk enabled her to rest assured that Diana's money worries would be short-lived.

CHAPTER TWO

Son-of-a-biscuit-eater, Rebecca mouthed silently. He's late. He's broken the first rule of making a good impression on a woman. And she felt certain J. C. Wheeler wouldn't even have the manners to think up a phony excuse.

Rebecca glanced around the receiving area and decided she should have tape-recorded her pep talk from yesterday for future use. How did Diana expect her to change rhinestones into diamonds when that rock-head was still buried somewhere on the side of a mountain?

After shifting from one well-shod foot to the other while she waited another fifteen minutes without being met by the reclusive J. C. Wheeler, she'd decided to collect her luggage and try her luck at the front entrance.

"So help me, if he doesn't arrive I'm going to find his secret little hidey-hole and blab it to the newspapers!"

Irritated by his tardiness, she opened her luggage carrier with a sharp snap. Other passengers' luggage circled lazily on the carousel while she watched for her two green suitcases, cosmetic case, and boxes to arrive from the airplane. Several seconds passed without anything popping through the opening.

A seasoned traveler, she'd always dreaded the possibility of arriving at a destination without her belongings. Terrific, Rebecca groaned, the airplane ate my dishes and clothing. Now what am I going to do?

She glanced at the clothing she wore. Her mint-green slacks and matching silk blouse looked impeccable. The forest-green sweater, whose arms were fashionably looped and tied across her shoulders, would afford her warmth against the nippy late-spring temperature, but she'd need her lined leather coat once the sun set.

Relief flooded through her when she saw one of the boxes she'd carefully packed nudge through the entrance. Turned sideways, the box wedged in the opening. Rebecca rushed forward. Just as she reached for the box filled with china and crystal, her largest piece of luggage slammed through the hole as though jet-propelled. Horrified, eyes rounded, she watched helplessly. The weighty weekend case landed squarely on top of the dish container. In what seemed like slow motion, the box shuddered and flattened with a resounding tinkle of broken glass.

Rebecca seldom cursed, but several explicit words hovered on the tip of her tongue. *Ladies don't curse, regardless of the circumstances,* echoed from her past. Automatically she responded to the cue by lightly biting her tongue.

"Need some help?" a booming voice inquired from immediately behind her.

Yanking the suitcase from the revolving carousel she clenched her teeth to keep from snapping, "Hell, no. You're too late to help." Instead she eased the suitcase to the floor and forced herself to smile. She turned to thank the man who'd kindly offered to come to her assistance. Her eyes slowly climbed from the third button of a bright red plaid flannel shirt, up to a bushy black beard and drooping mustache, to a pair of black eyes that were brimming with amusement.

While her eyes continued upward to his dark, tousled hair, his eyes leisurely roamed in a southerly direction. Rebecca was caught between the urge to restore an errant forelock into place and pulling it out, roots and all.

"Lesson number one, Mr. Wheeler. Gentlemen are always on time," she instructed icily.

Identifying him had the immediate effect she'd desired. His mouth parted slightly. The amusement in his rakish eyes died an immediate death. A fringe of inch-long eyelashes lowered fractionally as J. C. Wheeler studied the woman as though she were a rock specimen.

"You're Miss Prim and Proper?" he asked, his voice lowered to a hush.

"Rebecca Sterling," she replied, extending her hand. "Diana sent me."

His hidden smile thinned into a straight line. Rebecca Sterling wasn't what he'd expected. When he'd entered the luggage area, he'd scanned the area for a straitlaced woman, but had been distracted by a sexy blonde having difficulty. He wondered what her response would have been if he'd given in to the impulse to pop the provocative tush swaying in the air as she bent over to grab her suitcase. Undoubtedly, she'd have slapped his face, if she was what she claimed to be—a lady. John reserved final judgment, but the fire shooting from her sapphire blue eyes led him to believe she just damned well might be the kind of woman who'd have enjoyed it.

John swiped his right hand down the side seam of his jeans, then took her small slender hand, wondering what to do with it. By merely tightening his hand, he could drive her to her knees. Did she expect him to do something fa-de-da like kissing it? He glanced around to make certain no one was watching.

He's nervous, Rebecca deduced. A wicked glint lit her eyes. He'd probably jump right out of his skin if I brushed a finger across his love line. Surprised by the wayward thought, she hastily removed her hand. Was that a small sigh of relief she heard?

Uneasy with his masculine response to her slightest touch, John shifted his weight from one foot to the other. His heart thudded loudly in his chest. He could feel his ears turning red. A lady isn't supposed to cause that reaction, he condemned. Aloud he said, "We'd better get going if you're who you say you are."

"Would you care to see some identification? Driver's license? Credit cards?" She paused for effect. "Blindfold?"

Smart-mouth, John thought, certain a *real* lady would find him too intimidating for such snappy questions. He turned toward the exit, expecting her to follow him. "Guess you're who you say you are if you know about the blindfold. You don't have to wear it until we're in the Bronco."

"Stop right where you are, Mr. Wheeler," she ordered quietly in what she referred to as her "schoolteacher's voice." "We're going to get something straightened out, right now. I'm doing an old friend a favor by coming here to help you. I expect—."

John raised his hands to halt her rebuke. "Listen, lady." *And I use the term loosely.* "I paid Miss Feldman cold, hard cash to find me a woman to marry. She insisted on your coming here, not me."

"Do you really expect a lady, the kind of lady

31

you specified, to take a second look at you?" The question blurted out before Rebecca stopped long enough to tactfully rephrase it. "I mean . . ."

"Are you callin' me ugly?" he demanded, leaning toward her, wishing to God she were homely as sin.

"Unkempt," she replied sweetly. Lying through her teeth, she added, "I'm certain beneath the hair on your face you're as handsome as . . ." She hesitated, searching her mind for a Hollywood name that he'd recognize. Inwardly she cringed when his hand shot protectively to his face. She could almost hear him refusing to shave.

"King Kong?" He scratched his jaw. No point in telling her he shaved every summer. His beard was a blessing in the sub-zero temperatures, but it itched like crazy in the heat.

"A gentleman allows a lady to finish her sentence," she corrected. Her memory supplied her with the name of a dark haired, dark-eyed man that surely even J. C. Wheeler had heard of. "Clark Gable?"

John tried to keep from grinning, but failed. "I wished you'd have picked someone who hasn't been dead for fifteen or so years."

"And I wish you'd pick up my luggage and lead the way," she said, chuckling at his ready wit. Maybe she'd discovered John's saving grace. Humor appealed to most women. If he could keep a woman laughing, she might forget his lack of manners.

He inventoried the luggage and boxes on the revolving carrier with disdain. "All that's yours? How long do you plan on staying?"

"Until the job is completed," she replied, wondering if she'd live that long. "I'll carry the cosmetic case and the boxes on my cart."

Without being asked, John picked up the largest box and placed it on the cart. "What's in here? Lead?"

"Books." Much to her chagrin, Rebecca found herself closely scrutinizing the fabric covering his muscular shoulders. Another saving grace, she mused appreciatively. Generally speaking, women were attracted to a man with broad shoulders and narrow hips.

"I could have gotten books through the mail," John blustered.

"Hands-on learning during the day; homework at night."

John nearly dropped the cosmetic case when he heard "hands on." What kind of lady openly talked about putting her hands on a man? A real lady would unwillingly submit to a man's lusty nature because that was her duty. His blood stirred with anticipation as he predicted what she meant by "homework."

Surreptitiously, he watched Rebecca bend her knees rather than bend at the waist when she picked up the handle of the cart. She started toward the exit with long-legged, confident steps.

Ladies take little-bitty steps, he thought, shaking his head.

It wasn't that he objected to having a sexy woman share his house. Rebecca Sterling wouldn't be the first woman in his bed. It's just that he had set certain goals for himself that didn't include taking time out for a little fun and games.

Last winter, when the snow had been neck high to a moose, he'd decided it was time to find a woman to keep him warm on those long, cold, lonely nights. Somebody permanent. A lady.

Miss Sterling was no lady.

He didn't know exactly how to classify her, but any man who could see beyond his nose would agree that Rebecca looked like the kind of woman who'd purr like a kitten if a man stroked her silver-gold hair. She'd rub up against him, fitting those voluptuous breasts of hers against his chest, twining her legs around his . . .

"Well?"

John jerked upright. His mouth was too dry for speech. Rebecca was grinning at him as though privy to his thoughts. Dad blast the woman! She might look like a sexy kitten, but he knew about women who disguised themselves as ladies. They were skunks. Gold diggers. If she did marry a man, when the going got tough, she'd get going—straight for the bright lights of the city. She'd bleed him emotionally dry, pick his pockets for gold, then skedaddle back to a life of luxury.

Rebecca saw his curt nod. Her smile faded somewhat under his ominous glare. After he'd caught up with her, she tried to initiate a friendly conversation. "So where do you live, John?"

"Outside of town," he replied evasively. He steered her toward the ramp leading to his Bronco. "Once we're outside city limits, you'll have to wear the blindfold."

Pretending not to know about his profession and life-style, she asked, "Why blindfold me?"

"Because I don't want you to know where I live."

His succinct bluntness offended Rebecca. What did he think she was going to do? Rob him? Stake a claim on his mine?

But Rebecca reminded herself to hold her explosive temper in check. He didn't know the minute Diana had mentioned his name she'd recognized it and knew how he'd earned his considerable wealth.

"You can trust me not to—"

His curt snort cut her off. "Nobody knows where I live."

"Oh, yeah? That must be inconvenient for the mailman," she quipped, hoping he'd laugh and forget about the blindfold. She thought she saw his mouth twitch with humor, but couldn't be certain because of his scraggly mustache.

Gesturing toward the end of the row, John avoided a direct reply. "That's my Bronco."

"I could have guessed that," she muttered under her breath when she laid eyes on the dust-covered vehicle. Dents peppered the hood; the fenders were badly scraped. Windshield-wiper tracks revealed a cracked windshield.

She wheeled the cart to the back of the Bronco, then moved to the passenger's side and waited for him to open the door.

John made quick work of stowing her gear. He unlocked his door, slid in, then reached across the seat and unlocked her door. He glanced through the window. The look on her face reminded him of the first time his father had insisted he be a man and take a bite of spinach. He'd smiled grimly to keep from gagging.

What was wrong with her?

"Open the door, please," she instructed. "A gentleman opens doors for a lady."

John shrugged. All the girls he knew had hopped in his truck, wrapped an arm around his neck, and planted a kiss on his cheek. They weren't ladies, exactly, but at least they were strong enough to open a door. Or smart enough. He didn't know which, but he was certain Rebecca was both. With a heartfelt sigh, he reached for the door handle. Good thing he had long arms or he'd have had to get out and walk to the other side of the Bronco.

"Thank you. Next time, I'd appreciate your opening the door from the outside." She slammed the door to relieve the strain on her sharp tongue and flashed him a winning smile.

"You some sort of a mindreader?" he sputtered, feeling as though she'd plucked the thought right out of his brain.

"Intuition." She smiled, sincerely this time. Letting him think intuition was her source of information suited her plan to avoid wearing the blindfold. "A lady usually knows more about a man than he thinks she knows."

John started the engine. "Such as?"

"You live out in the boonies."

"That wasn't tough. Paved city streets aren't dusty."

"Your truck was damaged in a hail storm." Her guesses so far had been educated ones. She hoped her powers of observation would be as keen as her memory.

His right arm slid across the back of her seat as he turned to back out of the parking space. "Got the windshield, too."

He avoided looking her in the eye while telling a blatant lie. He justified his reply by minimizing the likelihood of his having any dangerous situations occur in the future. As long as he kept Rebecca away from the mother lode she'd be out of harm's way. By now the person skulking after him should have been thrown off course. If not, he'd think up some excuse to leave Rebecca at the house while he and Jennifer led the claim-jumper on a wild goose chase.

A thin smile played on his lips when he thought of Jennifer's reaction to having Rebecca on the property Jenny considered home. She wouldn't like having a city slicker who didn't know the difference between sapphires and blue rhinestones tagging along with them, either.

His mind was still on Jennifer when his fingers accidentally brushed against Rebecca's silver-blond hair. No comparison between the two, John mused. Jennifer's mane was black; Rebecca's mane was sun-dappled, a magical blend of sunshine and moonlight. Jenny's hair was wild and unkempt; Rebecca's was neatly cut at shoulder length. Inwardly he groaned at the comparison, feeling as if he'd had Jenny land a quick kick in his solar plexus. His Jenny would definitely be jealous of his attraction to Rebecca.

He removed his hand, shifted, then backed the Bronco out of the parking place. A full-fledged grin parted his lips when he noticed how close his hand was to Rebecca's leg. Come on, John, he silently chastised, you haven't had the urge to sneak a feel since you were sixteen. Shape up.

Rebecca swallowed, acutely aware of the mountain man's closeness. "Uhh, yes, well—my next guess is that you're some sort of prospector. Right?"

John slammed on the brakes. In one fluid motion his arm raised protectively between Rebecca's body and the dashboard. Every hair on his arm stood on end when the untimely stop propelled the soft swell of her breasts against his forearm. "I'll take a look at your driver's license, lady. Now."

"What?" she squawked as she was pitched forward, then backward.

"You heard me." His black eyes cut through her as though he were staring at her through a jeweler's loupe inspecting her for flaws. "Woman's intuition is one thing, but knowing too much is another. I may be ignorant in city ways, but I'm not stupid. Who are you? A reporter?"

"No. I'm not a reporter. Diana sent me." Seeing the dangerous glint in his eyes, she opened her purse and retrieved her license from her billfold. She thrust it toward him. "I am who I said I was."

He glanced at the picture, then at Rebecca. Satisfied that she hadn't lied to him, he returned her license. Rebecca was staring at him as though he had grown two heads—one wild and one crazy. Dammit, he silently cursed, between those reporters snooping around his homesite and the mysterious happenings during his last trip, he was acting downright paranoid.

To make amends for doubting her, he said, "Okay. You are who you say you are. Sorry I slammed the brakes on."

Rebecca realized when the apology caused his voice to crack that John Wheeler wasn't used to being wrong. His sincerity took the edge off her temper before she felt it necessary to gnaw on the inside of her cheeks to maintain her composure.

"Apology accepted, Mr. Wheeler," she replied with as much good grace as she could muster. "Perhaps, since we'll be leaving town, we should consider buying appropriate clothing first."

John's eyes skimmed over her pale green outfit. Maybe she's brighter than I thought she was, he decided magnanimously. She must have realized that a man couldn't spend twenty-four hours cooped up in a house learning how to bow and kowtow to a lady. The clothing she had on wouldn't last fifteen minutes even on a sedate walk around his property.

"There's a dry-goods store on the main drag out of town. We'll stop there and pick up what we need."

Hoping a "dry-goods store" was a quaint, old-fashioned nickname for the local version of Saks Fifth Avenue, she nodded her head. She paid little attention to where they were going after he paid the parking ticket. Her mind centered on what would constitute a basic wardrobe. He needed at least two suits. One navy, one silver gray, she decided after considering his dark coloring. Several shirts of various colors. White-on-white, pale blue, mellow yellow, she mused.

She'd tallied up her shopping list when she noticed they'd pulled off the street in front of a western clothing warehouse store. Good Lord, did he want one of those western suits with the wide, pointed yoke's in the front and back? She shook her head.

"This isn't what I had in mind. Isn't there a major department store in Billings?"

"Yeah, but I don't know why you'd want to pay twice the price for what you need."

"The price is unimportant." She shot him a polite smile. "You get what you pay for. Quality clothing is seldom overpriced."

"Yep," he drawled, opening his door and dismounting. "I couldn't agree with you more."

"Yessss," she corrected, too late. She'd noticed that his speech pattern was satisfactory earlier, but this yep, yep, yep had to stop. He couldn't date socialites in Denver sounding as though he were rounding up a bunch of wayward heifers.

John opened her door. He mocked the unnecessary gesture by casting her a rakish grin, then bowing at the waist and flinging his arm in the direction of the store. "Your charge card awaits," he gibed good-naturedly.

"*Your* charge card," she averred. "I left mine in Denver."

41

She expected him to pay for her new clothing? He realized he didn't know enough to fill a porcelain teacup about ladies and their finances, but he felt fairly certain a real lady wouldn't allow a virtual stranger to buy her clothing. He slammed the door and stalked toward the store. Rebecca Sterling might be an expert on how to train a gentleman, but she wasn't a lady herself.

Hands on her hips, Rebecca balked for two reasons. She wasn't about to run to keep up with him and he'd surprised her by expecting her to charge his new clothing on her expense account. Granted, she could submit the receipts to Diana and be reimbursed, but why bother?

Halfway to the door, John realized Rebecca wasn't beside him. He glanced over his shoulder. His steps slowed to a shuffle. He'd done something wrong again. He could tell by the placement of her hands on her narrow hips, and the expression on her face. Muttering an explicit remark, he turned and started back toward her.

"What'd I do wrong this time?"

"A gentleman slows down for a lady."

"And?" He could tell she hadn't finished her lecture by the sickeningly sweet tone of her voice. She'd have him hating sugar if she kept it up.

"I'm not paying for any clothes you purchase."

"I wouldn't expect you to pay for my clothes," he growled, his masculinity offended by her assumption. "But to be honest with you, I don't see what difference there is between me paying for your clothing and you paying for mine."

For a moment Rebecca didn't follow his logic. When she did, she sank her front teeth squarely into the tip of her tongue. Did he truly believe she'd suggested they stop to buy clothing for her? She clamped her teeth harder when she realized what he must have thought when she alluded to stopping at an expensive store. What kind of woman did he think she was? A gold digger?

Diana had warned her of John's apparent dislike for gold diggers. Stung that he'd placed her in that category, she wanted to lambast him verbally. Her self-control was being tested to the limits. She was tempted to verify the theory she'd made while in Switzerland: scratch the sugar-coated surface of a lady and underneath you'll find rock-hard candy.

"We are here to shop for you." Her teeth remained clenched, but the words were softly spoken. That's the best she could do under the circumstances.

Comprehending his major mistake, but wanting to cover it up, John replied, "Well, at least I was smart enough to pick the right store."

"Are you insinuating that I'm not very bright?"

One more bite and the tip of her tongue would be severed.

John grinned to conceal his dismay. He felt

like a man who'd was digging his grave with his own mouth. Her sapphire-colored eyes appeared hard and brilliant. He considered making some off-handed remark about men not expecting blondes to be mental giants, but decided against it. One person knowing his whereabouts was one too many. They'd come this far. He wasn't about to say something that would have her hightailing it out of Montana.

John blinked, trying to appear innocent. Remembering how she'd backtracked when he'd called himself ugly and she'd kindheartedly change his word to unkempt, he decided he'd better try a similar ploy.

He adopted a sheepish stance and said, "You? Dumb? Why Miss Sterling, you're just about the smartest woman I've ever met."

That was close enough to the truth to be convincing. He hadn't socialized with many women. Five to be exact—including Jennifer, and he wasn't certain she could be counted.

For good measure he added, "Heck, ma'am, I'm the one who's the ignorant rock-picker."

Rebecca's eyes narrowed. She raised her chin a fraction of an inch. She couldn't have agreed more, but didn't. John Wheeler was uncut, unpolished, and lacking in manners. But it was her job to change him.

She'd heard his pretty compliment regarding her intelligence, but her tongue remained sharpened, ready for action. The abrasive effect he had on her volatile temper made her wonder who was about to be changed, John Wheeler or Rebecca Sterling? Denim or silk? Which could survive an acid test?

An irreverent thought skittered across her mind from her past. Years ago she'd changed from pristine cotton underwear to silk. Denim underwear would be decidedly uncomfortable— even for a lady!

CHAPTER THREE

"Mr. Wheeler—"

"John," he prompted, wondering how long she could remain puffed up with hot air without bursting. "Or J.C."

"Okay . . . John." She adopted her best schoolmarmish voice to counteract the effect of his magnetic pull. He was rough around the edges, but he had a certain charm that was difficult to resist. "We're two strangers brought together for business purposes. Because we don't know each other we can expect to have—misunderstandings. Needless to say, I can't help you unless we establish the trust necessary between a teacher and a pupil, be forthright with each other."

John rocked back on the heels of his western boots. "Are you talking about shootin' straight with each other?"

"Precisely."

"Okay. I'll buy that." If she wanted straight

shooting, he'd set his sights directly at the cause of their misunderstandings and fire point blank. Either she was a lady or she was a woman. He'd give her a foolproof test. A lady might or might not wear slacks, but he knew exactly how a real lady would react to putting on a pair of denim jeans. A genuine, white lace and violet perfume lady would curl up her toes and die. "Those fancy pants of yours aren't going to last five minutes in rough country. You can get me all dandified when I arrive in Denver, but you're going to have to get some blue jeans before we leave Billings."

"Jeans are for mucking out stalls," Rebecca replied, quoting one of her Swiss teachers.

John grinned from ear to ear. She'd passed his test. Miss Rebecca Sterling wouldn't be caught dead in a pair of jeans. That was good enough for him.

"Well, since we can't buy what I need here and you feel as though you don't need anything, I guess we'd better mosey on down the road." He started toward his side of the Bronco when he heard her clear her throat. Making an abrupt one-hundred-and-eighty-degree turn, he opened her door.

"Thank you." Rebecca settled into the seat and smiled, silently congratulating herself. In less than ten minutes, they'd cleared the air of distrust and misunderstandings. By refusing to change her style of clothing, she proved to John that she was her own woman, trustworthy, and thoroughly competent. For all practical purposes she could think of John as just another one of Diana's clients. She'd do her job and then be merrily on her way.

One sideways glance at John's profile instantly undid the neat, tidy bundle of emotions she'd just placed a bow ribbon around. Deep down, she knew she was breaking her own rule about being forthright. Because as much as she tried to hide it, she was attracted to him, and right now, a business relationship was not all she had on her mind.

Besides, if he was attractive to her now, how was she going to react after she'd molded him into a perfect gentleman? Could she ignore her frustrated libido's loud grumblings? Dissatisfied with being unable to answer the questions without lying to herself, she directed her attention on the center line of the highway. Her eyes began to droop, hypnotized by the rhythmical flashes of white.

John faked a yawn. "Traveling always wears me out. Guess you're kind of tired, too, huh?"

"A little," she admitted, politely covering her mouth, knowing his yawn was contagious.

"Why don't you crawl over the back of the seat, curl up, and take a nap?" he suggested.

Rebecca heard a shadow of anxiety in his

voice. She opened her left eye for visible verification. His hands had tightened on the steering wheel. Beneath his beard she could tell a small muscle was nervously working.

We must be getting close to the first turn-off, she deduced. He'd told her that she'd have to wear the blindfold after they turned off the main highway. Was he going to insist? Since then, they'd spoken of trusting each other, but she knew trust had to be earned. Rather than put stress on the fragile bonds of their truce, she replied, "Thanks for the offer. If you don't mind, I'll stay where I am and doze. How much longer will we be traveling?"

"Several hours."

She considered stretching out on the bench seat, but decided the proximity of her head and his lap would be too tempting to her libido. "It'll be dark by the time we get there?"

"Hmm," he replied noncommittally. He'd lived in isolation too many years to reveal an exact location—even to someone he was beginning to trust. What time they arrived depended on how many diversionary side roads he chose to take. As the crow flies, his house was within three hours of Billings.

Rebecca closed her eyes and snuggled deeper into the seat. Prying information out of him was as difficult as engraving a piece of pure crystal and then filling the depressions with gold and enamel. Reminded of work, her fingers raised reflexively to the lapel of her dress, to the small gold piece of jewelry pinned to her collar. She loved the feel of its polished gold trunk that led to the enameled branches of the oak tree. There was no need to open her eyes. She could almost feel the cool leafy green color.

Hours later, deep in sleep, Rebecca felt herself falling. Disoriented by the violent rocking, she grabbed for the edge of her bed. Her eyelids sprang open when she felt a warm, hard, muscular thigh beneath her palm. She couldn't get her hand away fast enough to suit herself.

"Sorry," she blurted, pushing her hair back from her face and scooting back a respectable distance. Good Lord, she'd practically sprawled all over the man.

"My pleasure," John quipped with a cheeky grin. "I thought ladies were supposed to be damned door huggers."

Rebecca smoothed her skirt against her calves. "Even a lady isn't responsible for her actions when she's sound asleep," she bristled.

"Hang on tight. We're coming up to another gully."

She peered through the windshield into the darkness while bracing her hands on the dashboard. Her rear end lifted from the seat, at the same time her stomach lurched. All four wheels slammed into the road simultaneously. At any moment she fully expected to feel total loss of contact with the ground. John would probably say something inane like "Ooops, wrong turn," and they'd plummet down the side of a canyon.

"Slow down, for crissake. There isn't any road out there!"

"Can't slow down. This stretch is like a washboard. It would jar your teeth loose."

High beams of light from the truck pierced the darkness. Unexpectedly a boulder appeared from nowhere. Rocks crunched beneath the wheels as he swerved to miss it. "Are you sure you know where you're going?"

"Relax. I get lost with a road map in Denver, but I know my way around these rocks." He yanked the wheel to the left. "We're almost to the house."

In her estimation, John didn't have to worry about anyone crazy enough to follow him. They wouldn't be *able* to blab the location. She decided the wisest course was to keep her mouth shut—otherwise her tongue would be in dangerous peril of being bisected.

Glad to be home, John slammed on the brakes. "We're here," he announced with pride.

Rebecca sent a quick prayer of thanks heavenward. Eager to feel firm soil beneath her feet, she didn't wait for John to open her door. There was a time for good manners and a time for good sense.

He cut the lights and let her get her first impression by moonlight. John held his breath, waiting for her reaction. The architecture of his house didn't fall within the realms of a "typical" house.

Be tactful, she warned herself as her eyes scanned the monstrosity John lovingly called home. "It's . . . ah, interesting."

"Yeah, that's a pretty good description." He stepped beside her. "The house is situated in a blind canyon. Nobody gets in or gets out without me knowing about it."

"It's perfect for you." She tried to inject some enthusiasm into her voice, but failed miserably. What was the point of making John Wheeler the most eligible bachelor in Montana if he was doomed to live alone? The sneaking suspicion that no woman in her right mind would agree to marry him after she saw his house bothered her. She'd grown up being isolated from love. She hated the idea of John being self-condemned to a life of loneliness.

"You can't see much in the dark." Without premeditation, he looped his arm around her shoulder. "I started out building a log cabin."

In the dim light, she could see that one side of the structure had a wide veranda. The warmth coming from his slight hold on her shoulders had a peculiar effect on her. Without realizing it, the moment he'd drawn her close, she'd wrapped her arm around his waist as though they were the best of friends. She couldn't suddenly release him without offending him.

"By the time I'd hauled the logs and started building it, I decided the setting really demanded the house having a stone exterior."

Rebecca nodded toward the two-storied center section that reminded her of a castle's round tower. He started leading her toward a double door. She strained to find another appropriate comment. Finally, she settled for, "Hmm."

"Yep. But then long about the time the roof was being finished on the tower, I started thinking about getting married. Women prefer brick homes, don't they?"

"Hmm." That explained the slanted wing that projected to their left.

Before she could ask about the next section, John said, "Getting those bricks out here and finding a mason who could keep his mouth shut was a b-, b-, uh, a problem. I think he screwed up the original plan, because the house looked kinda lopsided. So I put the finishing touches on by building a second wing made of cedar that looked like the brick wing. Clever, huh?"

"Very." Tongue-in-cheek she added, "I've never seen anything quite like it. It's certainly an original."

John's chest expanded with pride. Sharing his house with Rebecca was . . . nice. Yeah, real nice, he mused silently. "Do you know my favorite thing about the house?"

"I haven't the vaguest idea." She was having difficulty giving the appearance of thoroughly appreciating his efforts. This was the kind of building that had to be every realtor's worst nightmare.

"It's like a precious gem. Regardless of what position you're in when you look at it—north, south, east, or west—you always get a spectacular view from the front porch. If this house were a diamond, it would be considered a high-quality fancy. Rare and expensive."

For the first time since setting eyes on the monstrosity, she could speak truthfully. "You're absolutely right. I don't think I've ever seen anything quite like it."

Rebecca's fragrance tantalized his nose. His open palm dangled precariously close to the fullness of her breast. Gracious almighty, she was tempting. Too damned tempting for a man who'd been without a woman for a long, long time. For half a second John wished he knew for certain she wasn't a real lady.

He removed his arm from her shoulders rather than risk having his face slapped. A man could only stand a certain amount of temptation. John was reaching his limit.

"Guess I'm not being much of a host, am I? I shouldn't be standing out here bragging about my house. I should be taking you inside and showing you around. Pick a door . . . any door."

"This one." Rebecca moved toward the arched wooden bridge in front of the castle entry. "It's irresistible."

John hoisted a box to his shoulder and picked up a piece of luggage. "Watch out for the ogre. Here I come."

Chuckling, she rushed ahead of him, opened the door and flipped on the light switch. Her chin literally dropped when the entryway seemed to explode into prisms of light that came from a huge, tiered crystal chandelier overhead. A stately staircase built of stone flecked with quartz curved along the rounded wall.

Rebecca glanced from the formal dining room on the right to the equally formal living room on the left. She wasn't familiar with antiques, but she felt certain the delicate tables and chairs were either originals or exquisite reproductions.

She had as much difficulty expressing herself inside as she'd had outside. "It's . . . grand . . . elegant . . . gorgeous. How in the world did you get the furniture out here?"

"Helicopter."

Tickled pink by the awed expression on her face, he hurried toward the stairs. He couldn't wait for her to see the bedroom.

"C'mon."

Dazed, Rebecca followed him.

"I had the bed imported from a derelict castle in Spain. It's really something." He unburdened his load and pushed open an ornately carved oak door. "Isn't this fantastic?"

Rebecca stood as though rooted to the thick carpet in the hallway. She'd seen pictures of platformed canopied beds with hand-carved headboards, but nothing compared to the magnificence in front of her. She entered the room slowly, as though stepping into a dream. Polished mahogany accented the marble-top washstand. A queen-sized armoire graced one wall; a Louis XIV desk balanced the room.

"Go ahead," John encouraged. "Jump on the bed. It's genuine goose down. Feels like you're sinking into a cloud."

"Jump on the bed?" she repeated, slightly appalled.

"Yeah, why not?"

Awestruck, Rebecca had strong reservations about touching it, much less jumping on it. "I couldn't. It's fit for a queen," she whispered reverently.

"Fit for a lady," John corrected. "It's all satin and lace and smells of lilacs, just like my second-grade teacher. She was a real lady."

Rebecca heard the wistfulness in his voice and turned in time to see his black eyes shimmer with longing. Now she knew whom he'd described in his letter to Diana. John Wheeler had for a model of a lady a woman he'd admired as a child.

John blinked. The image of Rebecca dressed in a long creamy high-necked satin gown stubbornly refused to vanish. He blinked again.

"Diana will find you a real lady," Rebecca answered, softly. "Maybe we'd better save this room for her."

"Unless you're superstitious, I just as soon you stayed in here."

"But . . ."

"No buts. You're my teacher. You like the room. It's yours for as long as you want it. I insist." Refusing to take no for an answer, John crossed to the open door. "I'll get your little suitcase and be back in a flash."

The half-hearted protest she was about to make came too slowly. The irresistible bed drew her closer. First she touched the oak leaf carving on the bedpost, then the satin coverlet. A small sigh hummed through her lips at the tactile pleasure she felt. Luscious. Her fingers pressed into the mattress. Heavenly. After the last few miles of the bone-jarring ride, she relished the thought of climbing between the sheets.

She glanced toward the door knowing she'd have to postpone going to bed. He hadn't been gone long, but she'd expected to hear him climbing the steps by now. She crossed to the door, stepped into the hall, and peered over the bannister.

"John?" Her voice echoed in the spacious tower. "John?"

Silence. The stone walls seemed to shrink, changing from a spacious stairwell into a prison. Goosebumps shivered down her arms.

"John! Where are you?"

Had he gone back to the truck? Maybe he thought she was hungry and was getting her something for them to eat. John was taking his role of host too seriously. Perhaps he didn't know that it was perfectly permissible for a guest to share in preparing a late-night snack.

Why didn't he answer?

Rebecca lightly ran down the stone steps. Her foot touched the landing just as she heard a loud boom. She was a city girl, but she'd watched enough television to recognize the sound of gunfire. "John!"

Thoughts of being out in the middle of nowhere without the vaguest idea of how to get back to the city had her heart pounding in her throat. She raced to the door and flung it open wide. Unable to see ten feet beyond her nose, she reached over and flipped up the switches. Floodlights shining directly on the entrance blinded her. Reflexively her forearm raised to protect her eyes.

An inhuman sound ripped through the silence,

petrifying Rebecca. Her vivid imagination took over for her paralyzed muscles.

Wild animals? Had John heard something—gone out to investigate and been attacked? Oh God, was he dead? Had he been eaten alive?

"Turn off the damned lights," John bellowed from behind the rear fender of the Bronco. "Get back in the house. Lock the door."

The welcome sound of his voice sent Rebecca running across the wooden planks. She wasn't going back inside the house by herself. Anything could happen to him and she'd be stuck in there . . . alone.

"Goldarnit, woman. Can't you follow orders?"

Rebecca screamed when John seemed to appear out of nowhere and snagged her wrist. Her body collided against his. Rebecca clung to him as though she were a mountain climber and he were a granite mountain.

All thoughts John entertained of pursuing the trespasser were forgotten. He leaned the rifle against the back of the Bronco. Whoever it was that had been sneaking around was long gone. Between Jenny and Rebecca, they'd raised enough of a ruckus to scare off the devil.

"What made that awful noise?" Rebecca whispered.

"My mule."

It sounded strange to his ears to call Jenny a mule. Jenny was more than a pack animal. Watch dog, companion, confidante, John thought, certain Jenny would twitch her long ears and nip at him for calling her anything less than his best friend.

"Didn't I hear a gun shot?" Rebecca's fingers shook as they smoothed the dimples her nails had made in his shirt.

"Nothing for you to worry about," John dismissed, not wanting to divulge information that might or might not be true. He'd been preoccupied when he glanced out the window. A coyote darting between the boulders on its nightly scavenging rounds could have been responsible for causing the shadows. But then again, those shadows could have been caused by a two-legged critter searching for something other than table scraps. Whatever it was, his buckshot had scared it off the premises. There wasn't any point in exciting Rebecca with pure speculation. "Just a night critter."

Besides, his nerves were jumpy enough for both of them. The tingling sensation her fingers caused as they tracked up the front of his shirt reminded him of how he felt right before he picked up a rock that Mother Nature disguised to look like a potato, but held sapphire crystals within. Was he on the verge of making a discovery more valuable than precious gems?

The thought scared him.

John wanted a lady he could put on a shelf and admire. The seductive signals shooting along his nerve endings warned him that the soft, cuddly person in his arms was more woman than lady.

He disengaged himself, took a step backward, and picked up his gun.

"Hungry?" he asked, searching for a way to stay near her but at the same time keep a respectable distance.

Rebecca's fingers curled around the empty night air. Being held in the security of John's arms had felt good—too good. She took a deep breath and answered, "No, but thanks."

For several seconds Rebecca stood toe to toe with John in silence. Good sense told her to bid him a quick good night and scamper inside, but for some unknown reason she wanted to linger. Why? What was it about those big black eyes of his that made her want to frame his beard with her hands and brush butterfly kisses along the arch of his brow? That didn't make sense. His height and breadth should have intimidated her, not made her want to cuddle against him.

What made her want to hold him and tell him everything would be all right? Why did she feel as though he were the person who was vulnerable? She was the one who'd been frightened by the sounds of gunshot and donkey braying. She was the one who'd been shaking in her boots. She was the one unaccustomed to her surroundings. And yet, she couldn't get rid of the feeling that John was the person in danger. Why? It didn't make sense to Rebecca.

Giving a perplexed sigh, she slowly turned toward the castle tower. Nothing could be solved tonight. Deciding these mysterious feelings she was experiencing must be delayed shock or merely the product of her overactive imagination, she started toward the door.

"Sweet dreams," came a whisper from behind her, sending pleasant shivers down her spine.

"You too," she replied.

Inside she picked up her cosmetic case and carried it with her upstairs. There had to be a reasonable explanation for the peculiar sensation in the pit of her stomach. She touched her forehead. No fever. No headache. No reason for her feet to sluggishly rise as though they contained lead.

Why did she have this intuitive feeling that she was headed in the wrong direction? She glanced down the curved staircase. There was nothing down there waiting for her.

She tossed her hair off her face and looked toward the bedroom. Nothing up there, either, she mused.

"I'm caught in limbo."

Shaking her head to dispel the peculiar notion, she hastened her steps. She wasn't caught in limbo going nowhere. She had definite goals set in front of her.

Tomorrow she'd begin at breakfast by introducing John to the fine art of eating like a gentleman.

CHAPTER FOUR

Sunshine streamed through the lead-crystal panes of the window as Rebecca put the final touches on her makeup. Dressed in navy blue slacks and a hand-crocheted pink top that accentuated her fair coloring, she completed the ensemble by clasping a necklace she'd made around her neck. A three-dimensional pink-enameled butterfly settled at the gentle swell between her breasts.

Mentally Rebecca prepared her morning lesson. First on the agenda, she had to check out John's table manners. She grimaced at the prospect. If his table manners matched his appearance, breakfast would extend beyond lunchtime.

"He probably eats everything with his fingers," she mumbled, then added, "No problem."

She'd worked with other clients who seldom used a knife and fork. Men raised in the city were addicted to hamburgers and french fries, neither of which required eating utensils. Unless John was a lip-smacking, fork-tapping belcher, she could teach him the simple rule of starting from the outside of the placement of silverware and working his way toward the plate. Since cocktail and salad forks weren't necessary for the first meal of the day, her task would be easy.

Rebecca opened her bedroom door and followed the aroma of coffee, bacon, and eggs. She sniffed her way down the staircase, through the formal living room, into a short corridor that led to another living room decorated in early American, into a country-style kitchen. John stood at the stove with his back turned to the doorway.

She started to say, "Good morning," but her jovial greeting was lost as her eyes skimmed from the damp hair at his nape, across his shoulders, down his narrowing torso, and lingered on his tight buttocks and long legs, before drifting to his bare feet. She swallowed. A lady certainly wouldn't have any complaints regarding his backside, she mused, grinning appreciatively.

With surprising agility for such a big man, he pivoted on the ball of one foot and faced her. Only by clamping her teeth together did Rebecca keep her chin from dropping. He'd shaved off the scraggly beard and mustache. His eyes seemed larger, darker, more inviting. Prominent cheekbones accentuated his square jaw line. But more beguiling than his black eyes was the tiny, Kirk Douglas dimple in his chin. Without it, his face would have been too perfect.

"Morning," he greeted, self-consciously raking his smooth-shaven face with the back of his hand.

"You shaved." Rebecca stated the obvious as though she'd discovered a vein of gold ten feet wide.

"Yep. I feel kind of naked. What do you think?" He wasn't conceited, but he knew the effect shedding his winter's beard had on women.

Rebecca inwardly groaned as she watched his mouth form the word "naked." What did she think? Lord have mercy, her first thought wasn't fit for polite company. Hot damn!!!—an expression from her pre–finishing school years—hovered on her lips. *Diana doesn't have a thing to worry about* was her second thought. Rapidly followed by—*What woman would notice how he eats?*

"I think . . ." Rebecca swallowed. "I think I smell the eggs burning." Considering the fact that her entire body seemed to be aflame, the smell could have been the soles of her shoes smoldering.

John removed the skillet from the burner. "Not yet, but they're close. How do you like yours?"

"Scrambled," she replied automatically. That way my eggs will have something in common with my brains, she silently derided.

"Hmm. I like mine over easy, but since you're company I'll do it your way."

She tilted her head to one side. Was that laughter she heard hiding behind his innocent comment? She focused her eyes on his mouth. Instantly she regretted her reflexive eye movement. Without the mustache his rakish grin stunned her.

Polite small talk provided a temporary defense. "I appreciate your consideration," she replied stiffly. What she needed was a strong cup of coffee. Caffeine would jolt the fuzzy edges off her tongue. Knowing she should wait until he offered her a cup didn't keep her from saying, "I'll help myself to a cup of coffee."

"The cups and saucers are in the cabinet to the right of the stove."

Rebecca moved beside him and reached for the dishes on the second shelf. "I'll set the table," she offered.

"Thanks."

John watched her as she raised her arms. Her blouse cupped the generous curve of her breasts. From his superior height he could see a hint of cleavage when the rounded neckline momentarily gaped. A pang of desire percolated through him. Teeth clenched, he concealed his reaction by leaning against the oven door.

Silently he blamed Rebecca for his uncomfortable predicament. A real lady would wear a blouse that buttoned up to her ears. Starched stiff as a board, he added for good measure. As she raised on tiptoe, his eyes were drawn to her derriere. The fabric of her slacks molded all too invitingly against her hips. What was that perfume she was wearing? A real lady smelled of violets and soap. Rebecca's fragrance reminded him of summer wildflowers—hot and untamed.

His eyes narrowed when he caught himself inching toward her. What would happen if he boldly pulled her into his arms? A lady would slap his face. What would she do? Was she a real lady or an imitation? Pure gold or fool's gold? Sapphires or glass?

Rebecca removed two plates, cups, and saucers from the shelf before John put his thoughts into action.

Embarrassed by their noisy clattering, she quickly moved away from John to the table by the window on the far side of the kitchen. She kept her eyes leveled on the coffee pot as she returned to the stove.

"Careful. The handle is hot," John warned a fraction of a second too late.

He dropped the spatula into the skillet and pushed it to a back burner when he saw her hand jerk back. Her eyes widened in pain. Grabbing her wrist he bodily hauled her to the sink. He held her hand under the faucet and turned on the cold water.

Rebecca inhaled as icy water splashed over the reddened skin. His after-shave lotion teased her nose, diverting her attention from her hand to the fact that she was being held snugly against his front. She could feel his wide belt buckle making an imprint on her back. Only the silky curtain of her hair kept their cheeks from touching. Tears of frustration pooled in her eyes.

John saw a tear track down her face when he gently brushed her hair back behind her ear. "That bad?"

"No. It's nothing." How could such large hands be so gentle? Why did she want to turn around in his arms and lay her head on his chest? Would he kiss the tears away? Feeling no pain, only his warmth, she babbled without thinking, "I hate doing something stupid so early in the morning. It sets the tone for the entire day."

His thumb skated over the sensitive underside of her arm. Seeing that she wasn't in pain, he teased, "Miss Prim and Proper isn't allowed to make a mistake?"

Rebecca held herself rigid. Although tempted, there wasn't a doubt in her mind that remaining encircled in his arms was a mistake that could result in something worse than a minor burn. A slight injury would heal in a matter of days. Intuition told her that John could inflict an injury that could last for years and years.

"No." Her weak, uncertain reply was both an answer to his question and a feeble protest against her growing awareness of John Wheeler as a man.

She shook her head as she turned off the faucet. She reached for a dish towel, but John's hand was faster than hers. He moved to her side. With utmost care he wiped droplets from the back of her hand, then dabbed her palm.

"Prospectors make mistakes. Sometimes we climb mountains and return empty-handed. Sometimes we think we've struck it rich and discover we've broken our backs lugging home fool's gold. But sometimes, if we're lucky, we find the real thing."

He placed her hand on the side of his face. His onyx eyes expanded as he wondered if he was mistaken about Rebecca being fool's gold. Her sapphire eyes held the hint of twin stars. Her lips were far more enticing than rubies. Slowly he lowered his lips toward hers.

Certain they'd both be making a mistake if they began the day with a kiss, Rebecca edged backward. She thought she saw the flicker of disappointment in his eyes, but decided it must have been an illusion. She'd barely had time to take a deep breath before he'd picked up a pot holder and coffee pot and sauntered across the kitchen.

"Cream? Sugar?"

He filled both cups.

"No, thanks." Annoyed that she'd let her imagination lead her astray, she forced a polite smile on her lips and asked, "Where are the knives and forks, napkins and tablecloth?"

"The silverware is in the drawer beside the sink." Silently John cursed the tremor in his hand that caused the coffee to splash into the saucer. "Paper towels are in the holder over the sink."

"Paper products are practical, but—"

"They're more than practical," he snapped, taking his frustration out on her. "Water is scarce here. It can't be wasted on washing napkins and tablecloths."

"Excuse me!" Rebecca sugar-coated her sarcasm with politeness. "Forget the napkins."

John strode across the room and slammed the coffee pot on the stove. His fingers curled around her upper arms. "I won't forget it . . . or what nearly happened less than five minutes ago. What are you, Rebecca Sterling? A lady? A tease? One of those city girls who gets their kicks by tantalizing country hicks?"

Taken back by his bluntness, her temper flared. She opened her mouth, then closed it. Chewing on the tip of her tongue wouldn't calm her. "A barbarian wouldn't recognize a lady if he had one in the palm of his hands."

"Maybe not," John conceded. His face tingled as though slapped. A gentleman would turn the other cheek; a barbarian would retaliate.

He confirmed her accusation by closing his mouth over hers.

72

Rebecca's common sense tangled with something unknown, something hot and hungry, something ferocious. The rational part of her mind told her to fight, kick his shins, scratch his eyes out. But neither her hands nor feet obeyed the command. Passion, an emotion she'd kept under tight control, surged through her hands. Her fingers gripped his shirt as she raised on her toes to diminish the difference in their heights.

Confused, she wondered what the female equivalent of a barbarian was called. Her response was anything but prim.

He'd expected a real slap. He'd braced for it. Instead she'd flowed over him like liquid gold poured into a mold. She met the gentle force of his lips with a force all her own. One that left him feeling stripped beyond nakedness. He felt vulnerable. Her hand on his chest had the impact of having reached inside and squeezed his heart.

For mind-shattering seconds, he forgot that he wanted a prim and proper lady. To hell with starch and violets. Now he only wanted the woman in his arms.

Rebecca was breathless when they drew apart. Her eyes fluttered as she valiantly tried to gain control over her emotional outburst. She fell back on her years of training for support. "Your manners need improving."

He could feel the passion that continued to vibrate between them. She failed miserably when she attempted to shoot him a cold glare. A small smile tugged at the corner of his mouth. "That's why you're here. Teach me to kiss like a gentleman."

"I wasn't hired for kissing lessons." Color tinted her cheeks. There wasn't a thing John could learn about kissing. His expertise still had her gasping for air.

"No steadfast rules a gentleman should follow?" he teased, loving the feel of her in his arms, refusing to allow her breathing space.

Annoyed by her desire to learn more about kissing from him, she frantically searched her memory for any prohibitive rules she'd been taught. Triumphant that she remembered one, she said, "Never kiss on the first date."

"Hmm." His lips hummed as they kissed her brow, her cheek, and nibbled their way down the side of her neck. He felt her resist momentarily, then arch her neck. Satisfied, he fluttered the lobe of her ear with the tip of his tongue and whispered, "On what date does a lady welcome me into her bed?"

Wondering if it was his tongue tickling her ear, or his audacity, that caused a bubble of laughter to gurgle between her lips, she replied, "On the day of the wedding."

"Never before breakfast?"

"Definitely, not B.C."

"B.C.?"

"Before coffee," she explained, moving from his arms to the table. John followed. He grinned, then shot her a delicious wink over the rim of his coffee cup. With any other student, she would have noticed that his long fingers were curled around the cup, ignoring the handle. She would have corrected the error. Her ears would have been attuned for the slightest slurping sound. John Wheeler could have poured his coffee into his saucer, blown on the steaming brew, and downed it. She wouldn't have noticed or cared.

His kiss had destroyed her objectivity.

Her kiss had blown *him* off his life's course.

John put his cup down and crossed to the stove as he mulled his realization over in his mind. Removing a platter from the cabinet, he put the bacon on one side and the eggs on the other, then put the platter in the microwave and set the timer. He slanted a glance at Rebecca.

She doesn't fit into my master plan, he mused. A man had to set goals or he'd lose his sense of direction. He'd learned that particular lesson the hard way by tagging along behind his father. Jacob Wheeler had aimlessly meandered from one mountain to another searching for precious metals. Gold fever, not a compass or a geological chart, dictated what direction he followed. There was no method to his madness.

"Boy, someday we're gonna strike it rich," was his father's daily litany. "We'll live in a great big house and find a little lady to take care of us." At sixteen, they were the last thing he heard when Jacob had peacefully slipped into a dream world and never returned.

The memory constricted the muscles in his chest.

Right then and there, he'd vowed to make his father's dream come true. He'd strike it rich. He'd have a home. He'd marry a real lady. But he wouldn't wait for the gods of good fortune to smile on him.

Three insurmountable obstacles loomed ominously between John and his goal: he was underaged, undereducated, and uncivilized. The first problem only time could cure. The second he'd corrected through self-education. Few books or magazine articles had been written about geology that he hadn't thoroughly studied. And last, but not least, Diana Feldman had hired Rebecca Sterling to make him socially acceptable.

None of his accomplishments had come easily. Without his single-minded determination he'd have failed. By keeping his objectives uppermost in his mind as he'd charged straight through the past fifteen years, he'd avoided being distracted by attractive alternatives. Now, when his ultimate goal was within easy reach, his eyes had strayed toward a provocative, sexy woman whose kisses caused a flash fire inside him.

76

Deep in thought, he wasn't aware of staring at Rebecca.

She was.

Rebecca intuitively knew he was silently waging war with himself. His black eyes unintentionally targeted the trace of pink lipstick on her cup. A similar smudge adorned his mouth. The kiss they'd shared had placed her smack dab in the center of his battlefield.

Rebecca, on the other hand, was fighting her own private skirmish.

Had it been less than forty-eight hours ago that she'd scoffed at Diana's matchmaking tactics? Diana admitted to toying with the idea of J. C. Wheeler being Mr. Right for her best friend. At the moment, Rebecca was doing more than playing with the idea; she was dissecting it.

From the time she'd laid eyes on his picture, she'd felt a tug on her heartstrings. She'd attributed the sensation to mild curiosity. After all, J. C. Wheeler was an enigma in her profession. Mystery and speculation surrounded every article written about the Montana hermit. When Diana had asked for a special favor, Rebecca had qualms, but she'd accepted the assignment. J. C. Wheeler wanted a wife and he had to brush up on his social skills to get one that met his specifications.

She glanced through the window, taking a sip

of coffee, wondering if loyalty to her friend would lead to losing her hard-won independence.

Marriage?

Her parents recommended it. That, and the example they'd provided, were enough to discourage her from romantic fantasies. On fleeting occasions, she'd considered it. Except for Diana all of her friends were married. Basically, she didn't have anything against marriage. She'd simply been too busy establishing her reputation as a goldsmith to seriously consider falling in love.

"Falling in love?" She mouthed the phrase toward the vast emptiness outside. "With J. C. Wheeler?"

He didn't fit the vague mental image of what the man she'd love would be like. The few men she'd dated were carbon copies of the type of men her friends had married: professional suburbanites with sophisticated tastes. No, she mused, John didn't fit her image of what she wanted any more than she fit the description he'd given Diana. He wasn't her Prince Charming; she wasn't his Cinderella. His bare foot would blister in wing-tipped shoes.

The microwave's timer buzzed, startling John. His eyes bounced from her cup on the table to the platter.

"More coffee?"

Platter in one hand and coffee pot in the other, he walked directly toward her. Whatever battle he'd fought, he won, if the smile on his face was any indication.

"Please." Matching his grin, she asked impishly, "Who won?"

His hand was steady as he refilled her cup. "Won?"

"The battle going on in your head," she said. "The devil or the angel?"

"Neither?" He paused, grinning. "Both? The hermit won."

Intrigued, Rebecca leaned forward. "Meaning?"

"Celibacy. It's something every hermit experiences, but he avoids it when there are other alternatives." He chuckled when her hand stopped midair as she reached for the platter. Sunlight danced wickedly in his dark eyes. "Isn't celibacy the nice word for doing without s-e-x?"

"Certain subjects aren't considered polite table talk," she answered in straitlaced fashion, while swallowing her laughter.

Taking the serving spoon from her hand before it fell, he scraped a healthy portion of eggs and bacon on her plate. "In that case, I guess discussing moving your suitcases into the master bedroom is out of the question, hmm?"

If suppressed chuckles contained calories, Rebecca knew he'd leave the breakfast table weighing a ton. Truth be known, she'd have gained a few pounds, too.

"Now who's being a tease?" she countered, tossing the accusation he'd made back in his face.

"I admit it. If I were a woman I'd be a tease," he conceded, chuckling as he emptied the platter onto his plate. "A favorite saying of the bad boys at the local pool hall is, 'If men were women, there'd be more whores in Montana.' "

Rebecca sealed her lips to control a bubble of laughter, then wiped them with her paper towel. Thoroughly distracted by the conversation, she'd failed to notice John had circled his plate with his arm as though his plate was a wagon train and the Indians were about to attack.

"You wouldn't be a lady?"

"A lady is what men marry, not what they dream about."

"Male logic," Rebecca groaned. While she'd been chasing her food around her plate with her fork, John had cleaned his plate. She forked a small bite of egg into her mouth, chewed thoughtfully, then swallowed. "I'd think a man would marry the woman in his dreams."

John tilted his chair, balancing his weight on the two back legs. His eyes devoured her as quickly as he'd eaten his food. Last night he'd dreamed of her. He'd awakened with the pillow clutched against his chest and the sheet twisted between his legs. For long minutes, he'd lain awake staring at the ceiling. Rather than fading into his subconscious, the dream vividly came to life in glorious Technicolor. His shaving had been prompted by the imaginary whisker burn his beard had left on her breasts. Rebecca Sterling was the kind of woman that played the leading role in a man's fantasies.

Rebecca didn't have to rely on intuition or mind reading to decipher the direction of his thoughts. Back in Denver a man's open admiration of her body would have embarrassed her. A city boy learned how to disguise his facial expressions by age twelve. John was in his thirties and there were moments when she could read him like an open book. What distressed her was her eagerness to turn the page to discover exactly where his thoughts would take both of them. The wistful expression on his face caused her nipples to harden; the tips puckered beneath his steady gaze. John Wheeler accomplished more with those black eyes of his than other men had achieved after several dates.

"Four on the floor," she said to draw his eyes from her revealing cotton top to his chair.

The chair's legs hit the floor with a thud. "I know better," he muttered, meaning he knew better than to openly stare at a woman. He picked up his plate and took it to the sink.

Rebecca wasn't certain she knew exactly to what he referred, but she wasn't going to risk asking him for fear of how he'd respond. His direct reply would devastate her intention to avoid making another dire mistake.

Stick to teaching him table manners, she silently warned herself, *You'll be less likely to get burned that way.*

"Unless you've been excused, you're supposed to stay until everyone has finished."

The bad boys at the pool hall had given him similar instructions. John grinned as he rinsed his plate with cold water. But they'd been talking about making love, not table manners. Grinning, he set the plate aside. The bad boys knew more about being a gentleman than he'd realized.

CHAPTER FIVE

John hunched over the table pretending to be fascinated by the clothing on the glossy pages of the men's fashion magazine. In actuality, from behind the fingers he'd lapped over his forehead, he watched Rebecca's graceful movements as she washed, dried, and put away the morning's dishes.

"Tell me when you see something interesting," she'd said.

He'd seen plenty he liked during the last ten minutes, but he hadn't opened his mouth or spoken a word. The starched, ruffled apron he'd insisted she wear was causing him silent agony. It shouldn't. He'd bought it because it reminded him of the apron his second-grade teacher had worn. How was he to know the perky bow at the back of her waist would accentuate her hourglass figure? The ruffled vee of the bib should have concealed the womanly thrust of her breasts as she raised her arms to put the plates in the cupboard.

He'd mentally calculated there was just enough room to slide his arms between the starched fabric and the softness of her blouse.

Rebecca listened for the sound of pages being turned as she dried the skillet. All she heard was her heartbeat pounding in her ears. She could feel those black eyes of his freely roaming from her shoulder blades to the back of her knees. Only by biting her tongue had she quelled the urge to fill the silence with inane chatter.

Above all else, she couldn't let John Wheeler know the effect he had on her female hormones. When she'd let common sense prevail and stopped his mind-altering kisses, he'd accused her of being a tease.

What made him believe a woman was either a lady or a tramp? There was little doubt in her mind as to what John and his associates at the pool hall would think if she gave in to the desire to curl up on John's lap, twine her fingers in those dark waves of his hair, and kiss him until he was breathless.

She stooped to put the skillet in the bottom drawer of the stove. Was that a groan she heard? *His or mine?* she silently questioned. Slowly straightening, she glanced toward the table. Must have been me, she decided. John had his eyes glued to the pictures in the magazine.

John flipped the page and blindly pointed toward the picture of a model in formal evening wear posed in front of a glitzy restaurant. "What do you think of this outfit?"

"You'd wear a sky-blue tuxedo with mauve satin lapels?" she inquired, moving until she stood behind him.

To cover his blunder, John moved his finger to the other man in the picture. "It's better than a pink suit with a purple shirt."

"True. But for your purposes, I'd recommend a well-tailored dark suit."

She started to reach over his shoulder to show him an example. At the same moment, John shifted his shoulder, turning toward her. His nose skittered across her apron front. Rebecca jumped backward as though she'd bumped into a live electrical wire.

To say he was sorry would have been a bold-faced lie. He'd have given a handful of uncut sapphires for her to have moved in the opposite direction. John tilted his head to one side; he gradually raised his eyes until they met hers. "Hermits don't bite," he teased.

"What about a barbarian?"

John grinned at her quick retort and eased to his feet. Now she was looking up instead of down her nose. He could think of a hundred ways she was superior to him, but his height diminished her advantage.

"Maybe a little nibble here and there. Nothing that would cause permanent damage."

"John . . ." His name caught in her throat, prohibiting a comeback. She counteracted with an indignant sniff.

"You did ask," he rebuked mildly as he playfully tapped the end of her nose with his forefinger. "Last night we agreed not to lie to each other, didn't we?"

Caught in a trap of her own making, Rebecca nodded her head. "What I should have said is—we need to be tactful with each other."

"Tactful? Is that a refined word for lying?"

"Not exactly. Ladies and gentlemen must be diplomatic for prudence's sake."

"Care to tell me how I could have been diplomatic with my face rubbing against—"

"You could have apologized."

John grinned. "I wasn't sorry." He ignored her haughty expression. "But, I guess I could have reacted the way you did: jump back, wrinkle my nose, and act miffed."

"Under the circumstances, I'd say my reaction was prudent," she said defensively. "What would the lady you described in your letter have done?"

His grin grew into a full-fledged smile. "Swooned?"

"Which would give you an excuse to catch her and carry her to the sofa?" Rebecca blinked twice to clear the image in her mind's eye of being swooped off her feet and carried masterfully in his arms. Instantly she understood why smelling

86

salts had been invented. A woman would need a good whiff of ammonia to inhibit her wayward inclinations.

"That idea appeals to me. In two seconds flat, I'd be right beside her."

"Wrong," she corrected with a smug smile. "You'd be rubbing the red handprint on the side of your face and picking yourself off the floor."

His fingers stroked his clean-shaven jaw as he contemplated her reply. He didn't like the idea of having his face slapped any more than he liked the idea of telling tactful little white lies to save face. He mused aloud, "Why can't a lady just say what she thinks and avoid all that rigmarole? I touch her—if she likes it, we go further. If she doesn't like it, she tells me to get lost."

"Why, John Wheeler, I do believe you've changed your mind about what kind of woman you're looking for." She circled him, looking him up and down as though she'd discovered a new man. "You've described perfectly how today's woman reacts. Shall I get hold of Diana and tell her you've changed your mind? Tell her to pitch your list?"

"No. Absolutely, no. I made up my mind years ago as to what kind of woman I wanted in my life. It's too late to change my plans."

Defeated when she thought she'd won her point, Rebecca muttered, "Don't confuse him with facts, he's made up his mind. You may not know the meaning of tactful, but you sure as heck know the meaning of stubborn."

"Hell, yes, I'm stubborn and proud of it. A stubborn man sets his sights on a goal and reaches it. I'd still be roaming around Montana picking up worthless rocks if I hadn't been stubborn." His eyes burned with intense determination. He'd made his master plan; he'd followed it. He was a rich man because of it. He'd be a damned fool to change at this late date. "You just tell me what it takes to win a lady. I'll learn how to open doors, to dress like a fop, and to tell little white lies with the best of them! Whatever it takes, I'll do it. Mark my words, Rebecca Sterling, I'm going to marry a real lady."

"So be it," Rebecca declared, knowing he'd be miserable if his stubbornness led him into a marriage with a dried-up stick of a woman. The hard glint in his eyes told her it was pointless to argue with him. She could be every bit as single-minded as John Wheeler. Her voice was sweeter than honey when she said, "We'll begin from the beginning. Go outside and knock on the door. We'll assume that you're arriving on time and properly attired." She cast a meaningful glance at his bare toes. She fluttered her eyelashes and added, "You concentrate on polite small talk. I'll try to act like the *lady* you described in your letter."

Her insincerity earned her a glare from John. She'd irritated him. She was capable of dealing with anger. It was his mixed-up definition of a lady that made her blood boil.

She wiggled her fingers in a dismissive gesture, cooing, "Close the door quietly on your way out, please."

Her smile deflected the daggers he shot over his shoulder in her direction. He yanked the door open, stepped outside and soundlessly closed the door. A whisper would have been louder.

Rock samples gouging the soles of his feet diverted his anger. His eyes flew from the floor of the porch to the sack on the wooden table. Day before yesterday it had held his latest findings. Someone had emptied the contents, carelessly scattering his samples hither and yon.

John kicked the rocks from under his feet and moved to the railing. He hadn't imagined the moonlit shadows last night; someone *had* been out there skulking around. His eyes narrowed as he scanned the ridge of the canyon. The thought of someone sneaking around his property, handling his belongings, sent a chill shivering down his spine.

"Didn't find what you were looking for, did you?" John mumbled. A thief could search the house from dawn until doomsday and wouldn't find what they were looking for—a star sapphire as big as a robin's egg.

Publicity, he silently growled, his fingers gripping the bannister.

Every newspaper in the country had picked up on the story of the hermit who'd found a stone worth a king's ransom. At the time he'd actually laughed when he read about J. C. Wheeler, mountainman with the Midas touch, who turned a Montana boulder into star sapphire. Nobody would believe that hogwash.

One diligent reporter didn't. He nosed around until he pieced together all the facts. J. C. Wheeler had found more than one star sapphire. He'd sold several. Comparatively speaking, the stones he'd sold were smaller, but nonetheless perfect. Valuable.

His laughter stopped when people feverishly began to ask, "Are there more? If so, where?"

That's when the nightmare began.

Nice people changed into monsters. At night, shadowy figures dogged his footsteps. In broad daylight, strangers would stop him in the middle of the street to ask him pertinent questions. Where'd you find them? What do they look like when you pick them off the ground? How many do you have? Do you want a partner? Could you draw a map?

He remembered the hard, greedy look that would come into the eyes of the person asking the questions. Star-sapphire fever, he'd called it. Once a good person was afflicted with it they didn't want to hear about physical hardships, or loneliness, or fatigue. They wanted one thing. To be taken to the area where he'd struck it rich.

When he refused to lead sapphire-hunting expeditions, disappointment fueled the fever. Burning brightly, the fever caused the victim to act irrationally. Their voices raised to a high pitch as they asked, "How come you're so selfish? Would it hurt you to share the wealth? Isn't there plenty out there for everybody?"

To get away from the feeling of being crowded into a sardine can, he'd packed his meager belongings and gone on a mountain fishing trip. The hook and sinker had barely splashed into the isolated stream when people started appearing out of nowhere. Men, women, and children grinned at him as they panned the creek, searching for instant wealth. He didn't stick around long enough for the icy water to fade their smiles. They'd all get the fever.

He backpacked into the mountains and stayed until winter.

If he hadn't been a hermit to begin with, he would have become one.

He ended the nightmare by refusing to talk to the press, by sticking his hand in front of the camera when a reporter tried to take his picture. Gradually most people forgot what he looked like. He could drift from one town to another without causing a stir. Finally, he'd come home.

John released the rail and rubbed his eyes with

the heel of his hand. He'd buried those unpleasant memories. Almost everyone he'd met in the last couple of years were hard-working, God-fearing people like himself. Few people could pinpoint the location of his home; he'd intimidated those who could into respecting his privacy.

With one pint-sized exception, he thought, turning toward the door. Rebecca stood up to him as though she were twice his size and three times as ornery. Fierce scowls and flexing his muscles would amuse her rather than having the opposite effect.

While John silently debated the possibility of Rebecca being susceptible to star-sapphire fever, she was impatiently awaiting her cue to open the door.

His habit of taking his own sweet time rankled. How long did it take for him to turn around and bang on the door? Surely he couldn't have gotten lost on his own front porch.

"Ready and waiting!" she called none too sweetly.

John stooped down and picked up two rock samples from the porch. One way or another he was going to find out how much Rebecca knew about him. He rapped his knuckles on the door frame, feeling damned silly for knocking at his own door.

"John Wheeler?" Playing her role to the hilt, she forced a radiant smile on her lips.

"Who'd you expect?" he snarled, stepping forward. He couldn't discover how much she knew by allowing her to treat him as a total stranger.

The door slammed in his face. From the other side, he heard Rebecca say, "Try again. Your misplaced sense of humor isn't going to impress a lady."

John stormed through the door. "Game time is over, Miss Sterling. Care to tell me how much you know about precious gems?"

Taken completely off guard, she thrust her chin forward defensively, but stood her ground. "Is this your idea of sociable small talk?"

"Someone picking through my rock samples has taken us past the small-talk stage. Before you came here, you knew who J. C. Wheeler was, didn't you? Yes or no?"

There was no getting around his question with idle chatter or little white lies. Despite his blustering, Rebecca knew John was harmless. "Yes, I did. So what?"

"So, why are you here? Did you and your accomplice think—"

Rebecca halted his accusation by closing the gap between them and tapping him in the center of his massive chest with her forefinger. "Stop right there. My knowing who you are doesn't implicate me in anything."

"Then why didn't you tell me straight out?" He brushed her finger aside as though it were a bothersome fly, and grasped her shoulders. "Why play that woman's intuition game while we were driving out here?"

Deciding he was going to shake the whole truth out of her if necessary, she braced her hands on his chest and blurted, "Because I felt certain that once I told you helping Diana Feldman was a side job, you'd start asking questions about my regular work. I'm a goldsmith who specializes in enameled jewelry, Mr. J. C. Wheeler. What are you going to make of that?"

"A damned strong case for kicking you right out of Montana," he replied, giving her shoulders a small shake. "What happened last night, Rebecca? Did you wait until I was asleep, then sneak through the house? You must have thought you'd hit pay dirt when you found the sack on the porch, huh? After you examined the specimens and found them worthless, you had the remainder of the night to think up a new plan of action. Was that kiss this morning part of the new plan? Just how much are you willing to do for a handful of star-sapphires?"

His insinuations hurt more than his grip on her shoulders. Rebecca looked him straight in the eye. "Nothing. Absolutely nothing. I'm here because an old friend needed help. I have no interest in star-sapphires."

"You expect me to be naïve enough to believe you?" His eyes searched hers for signs of deceit, for the greedy glow of sapphire fever. They were clear, unwavering. She was either telling the truth or she was a habitual liar. She didn't even blink.

"Yes."

Her quiet response defied him to doubt her innocence. Logically, he should. Before he'd contacted Diana Feldman, he hadn't been bothered. Since then, he'd been caught in a minor avalanche, spotted an intruder, and been burglarized. The circumstantial evidence was damning. Every piece of incriminating evidence pointed toward Diana and her friend, Rebecca.

And yet, something intangible made him believe in her innocence.

Rebecca instinctively knew the moment his hands dropped from her arms that he'd decided to trust her completely. She framed his face with her hands. "Someday soon, J. C. Wheeler, you're going to have enough confidence in yourself to know that you're more valuable than gemstones."

The strength he needed to draw away from Rebecca's light hold was almost painful. Just looking at her simultaneously pulled him in two directions: Get closer, while you can. Back off, before it's too late.

"I'm sorry," he murmured hoarsely.

Glad to hear the words that sounded rusty from disuse, Rebecca smiled her forgiveness.

CHAPTER SIX

"Does polite small talk include topics other than the weather and politics?" Following the path of John's eyes to the pink butterfly, Rebecca guessed where his question was leading. "Of course."

"Did you design your necklace?"

"Yes. What do you think of it?"

John lifted the delicate chain until the butterfly rested in the palm of his hand. His knuckles barely touched the sensitive hollow of her collarbone, but it was enough to remind her of the feel of his lips on hers. By tilting her face to one side, she'd be within easy kissing distance.

Steady, she silently ordered herself.

"It becomes you. Pretty, fragile-looking but solid."

"Thank you."

His hand skimmed lower as the butterfly slid between his fingers. He felt her warm breath flutter across the rugged planes of his face. His eyes raised to her parted lips. He wanted to kiss her, to touch the soft mounds sheltering the butterfly. "Lucky butterfly," he murmured.

She laughed. At least she tried to laugh, then spun away from him. "You don't waste much time on small talk."

"Jennifer never complains." From the puzzled look on her face, he could tell she'd forgotten about his mule. "She's the only female I've been around for any length of time."

Filled with undiluted jealousy, Rebecca bit her tongue. "Docile-natured" was one of the attributes he'd listed in his letter, so she tried to keep her cool. "Why haven't you married her?"

John grinned. "I'm fond of Jenny, but she's not the kind of female I could love, if you know what I mean."

"I know exactly what you mean." Her eyes narrowed. "Good enough to sleep with, but not refined enough to wed. She isn't your idea of a refined lady."

"Nope, but I wouldn't have enough gumption to say that to her face." *She'd kick the livin' daylights out of me.*

John tucked his thumbs under his wide belt and rocked back and forth on the heel of his boots. If he didn't know better, he'd swear those sapphire eyes of Rebecca's had turned the color of jade. Delighted with the thought of Rebecca being jealous, he added, "Jennifer has other good qualities, though. She's loyal, hard-working, sensitive . . . considering she's so blasted stubborn. No, Jenny isn't a lady, but she's all woman."

Peeved that he'd discuss another woman within seconds of almost kissing her, Rebecca snapped, "Gentlemen never kiss and tell."

"She wouldn't mind. She's the kind of woman who likes it when a man throws his arms around her neck or pats her on the fanny." John was having great difficulty keeping a straight face. "When she gets cantankerous I scratch her belly."

He scratches her stomach? Uh-huh. Why, he's pulling my leg! She hadn't seen a dog around anywhere, but she felt certain his sweet Jenny had four legs. The rat!

"Perhaps, since you're genuinely fond of Jenny, you'd consider letting her join us. Turning her into a lady won't be any more difficult than teaching you how to be a gentleman."

"Nope, I don't think she'd change. I'd feel bad about you wasting your time trying to teach her table manners. Poor Jenny can't even drink water without slopping it all over the floor. She'd just make an ass out of herself."

Now that she was listening for clues, Rebecca easily deciphered the hidden meaning. Jennifer was a jackass. Every prospector had a mule. She could have kicked herself for letting J. C. Wheeler bamboozle her.

"Some clients are more difficult than others,"

she said, oh so sweetly. "I remember one man who was particularly obstinate. I set a perfect example by being charming, witty, sympathetic, but he was a real son-of-a-biscuit-eater. You know the type. I'd hand him a magazine and he'd drag it into his cave and eat the cover."

John chuckled, knowing he'd overplayed his hand. He followed her as she strolled into the kitchen. "A primitive old goat, huh?"

"Not exactly. Old goats don't play practical jokes. He wasn't old, either. Actually, I'd say he was about your age." *And height, and weight.*

While she'd been talking, she'd also been opening drawers. She smiled brightly when she found what she'd been looking for. Crooking her finger, she beckoned John closer.

"I'd lay in bed at night, wondering what I was doing wrong. Why wasn't the beast cooperating? Lack of motivation? No, he'd paid Diana a premium price for my services. Lack of intelligence? No, that couldn't be the reason. He was very, very clever. Finally, I realized where I'd made my mistake."

"You'd mistaken an ass for a primitive old goat?" John offered, laughing shamelessly.

Rebecca fluttered her eyelashes, grabbed the front of his shirt in one hand and pulled a rolling pin from the drawer behind her with the other. "Uh-uh. I'd failed to get his attention. A few whacks smack dab between his eyes and he became as docile as a lamb."

"You wouldn't hit a man twice your size, would you?"

Lazily circling the rolling pin like a baseball player, she chortled, "Your size doesn't intimidate me, J. C. Wheeler. I'm small but quick."

John made a dash for the door. "Quick-tempered woman with a quick tongue. I'll bet Jennifer is faster on her feet than you are."

"You can run, but you can't hide," she jeered, hot on his heels. "I'm going to get you."

Once outside, John had the advantage. He ducked beside the house, crouched down behind a row of holly bushes, and waited. His low chuckles threatened to reveal his hiding place as he heard Rebecca fulminating.

She scanned the rim of the canyon. "He's probably halfway to Sacrifice Cliff," she simmered. Voice raised, she called, "Take a flying leap, would you?"

Barefooted, John moved quickly and quietly.

Before Rebecca's inner radar activated to sense his nearness, John slung one arm around her waist, lifted her from the ground and plucked the rolling pin from her hand. "Gotcha!"

"The heck you do. I didn't take a self-defense seminar for nothing!" She squirmed, jabbed him with her pointed elbow between his ribs, and landed on his big toe as he dropped her. Spinning around, she assumed a karate pose she'd seen in a recent movie. "How's that for getting your attention," she gloated.

The stunned look on his face as he hopped around on one foot destroyed her composure. Doubling over, she shook with laughter.

What a woman, John admired silently, wiggling his big toe. She hadn't hurt him, merely caught him unaware. Her melodious laughter soothed any damage to his male ego.

He folded his arm over his face. "You pack a helluva punch for a lady. I think you've ruined my career and my prospects for getting married. Who'd want a penniless mountain man hobbling beside her for the rest of her life?"

"Tell your sob story to Jennifer," Rebecca scoffed, grinning in triumph. "You'll get more sympathy from her."

His black eyes danced with merriment as he peeked over his sleeve. "Ladies are supposed to be sympathetic."

"Gentlemen don't attack from behind," she countered.

John grinned, grabbed her, and planted a smacking kiss on her saucy mouth.

"You're asking for it, John." Lips tingling, her breasts flattened against him, her arms wound around him, she wondered who was asking for what. His teasing, platonic kiss left her hungry for more.

Instantly, he raised his hands skyward, but his eyes strayed to her lips. "Sorry. I was trying to be a gentlemen . . . attacking from the front."

"You're impossible." Rebecca groaned. The hug she gave him was as fleeting as his kiss. "Utterly impossible."

"You have to give me credit for trying."

"You're trying, all right." She hesitated, wetting her lips with the tip of her tongue, inviting him to try again.

A loud series of hee-haws forestalled John from lowering his lips to hers. "Jenny is the jealous type," he whispered, half smiling. "She thinks I belong to her."

Wishing she could stake a similar claim, Rebecca cast a baleful glance in the direction of the barn. "Demanding, too."

John laced his fingers through hers and started toward the barn. "Stubborn, demanding, jealous —typical female."

"But ladies don't have those traits, do they?" he glibly deflected his taunt.

"No, they don't." He squeezed her hand. She watched his tongue roll around in his cheek, before he said, "Tell me, Rebecca, where did you learn to kick and punch? Charm school?"

"Swiss finishing school, actually. I graduated with honors." On paper, her qualification's were impeccable. Only the dean of women and her mother knew what an unruly rascal she'd been. "What about you?"

John winced. He had gotten caught in the verbal trap he had set for her. He wondered how Rebecca would react if he told her that his formal education ended in the sixth grade? Not wanting to risk lowering himself in her eyes, he swallowed the whole truth and doled out a portion of it. "I wasn't at the top of the class."

"I can't picture you at the bottom of anything —academic or otherwise."

Adopting a jaunty swagger to hide his feeling of vulnerability, he said, "I wasn't at the bottom, either."

"Mischief maker?" Rebecca asked, sensing his wariness.

"Me? No way. The principal didn't even know me by name."

She caught his slip of the tongue: colleges had deans; high schools had principals. For some strange reason she couldn't comprehend, he was sensitive about not attending college. Rebecca shrugged dismissively. Education was important, but it wasn't a ticket to paradise. Most of the professional men she knew would gladly have exchanged their rung on the corporate ladder for John's position in life.

"Calm down, Jenny. I'm coming." John unlaced his hand from Rebecca's and picked up a bucket. "She's complaining because I usually feed her first thing in the morning."

Rebecca watched him scoop pellets from a tin pail, then followed him inside. She blinked, adjusting her eyes to the dim interior. Stacks of sweet-smelling hay lined the back wall. To the left, she saw several large earth-moving machines. Jenny had to be in the stall to the right. Rebecca could hear her moving around, but couldn't see her.

John opened the stall door and dumped the bucket into a feeding trough. "Don't do it, Jenny. No tricks. You kick me and I'll turn Rebecca loose on you."

Like a finicky cat, Jenny ignored the warning and sauntered over to her feed. Her tufted tail twitched arrogantly.

"I thought mules were bigger," Rebecca said. "I guess I expected to see a horse with long ears."

"You're thinking of a Missouri mule. Jenny's a special breed." He pointed to the dark cross on her back, then stroked her flank. "According to legend, Jenny's lines date back to biblical times. Supposedly the reason mules are sterile is because Joseph's mule refused to move and kicked him. He put a curse on all mules saying that they should never have a father or mother of their own kind, or any children."

Looking at Jenny, who was peacefully munching her food, Rebecca's sympathies went out to the animal. "I can't believe I'm saying this about a mule, but she's a little darling. Sort of a miniature horse with big ears and a sassy tail."

"Whisper when you say m-u-l-e. Jenny thinks she's human." John chuckled. "Her looks are deceiving. Without provocation, she'll bite and kick. Believe me, it takes a firm hand to keep this woman in line."

"Do you think she'd let me pet her?"

Jenny answered for herself by pawing the floor, snapping her teeth, and flattening her ears backward.

"See? I told you she was ornery." Giving his mule a final pat he crossed to the door. The corners of Rebecca's lips were tugged downward in disappointment. He threaded his long fingers into her blond hair and tilted her face up to his. "I really hate to see you look so downhearted. I'm willing to make the supreme sacrifice. You can pet me."

The dirty look she shot him didn't faze his cocky grin. Hearing Jennifer's hoofs shuffling backward did. Before she could say, "Look out," John dodged. The mule adjusted her hindsight, and delivered a swift kick in the seat of his pants.

"Damn you, Jenny," John bellowed. "Branding me with your hoofprint doesn't mean I belong to you. Damned jealous female."

Jenny turned, brayed, and impudently swished her tail.

"I'm *not* going to turn the other cheek," John replied, as though he understood what the mule meant.

Rebecca clamped a hand over her mouth to stifle her giggle. Her eyes zoomed between irate man and seemingly unconcerned mule. Fascinated, she watched Jenny's inch-long, curly eyelash lower over her eye. Rebecca would have sworn on a stack of Bibles that the mule had winked at her.

"Ungrateful female," John muttered, stomping out of the stall and slamming the gate. Voicing his thoughts, as was his habit when he was around Jenny, he marched to the back of the barn and picked two leaflets of hay from an open bail, returned to the stall and tossed them inside. "Bites the hand that feeds her. Steps all over my feet. Keeps me up all night hee-hawing. Refuses to budge an inch if the load isn't balanced to her satisfaction."

Grinning, Rebecca supplemented his growing list of complaints. "Interrupts when you're about to kiss another female."

"Yeah. Interrupts when I'm about to kiss anooo . . . I said I *hugged* Jenny. I don't kiss her," he grumbled. "You're the only female I want to kiss!"

"Don't get mad at me because you've got female problems," Rebecca teased, gaily skipping out of the barn.

John raised his hands heavenward. "Why me, Lord? Wasn't one smartass enough?"

"Flattery won't get you anywhere," she called over her shoulder.

Rebecca felt as though her feet had sprouted wings as she flew across the yard.

You're the only female I want to kiss echoed in her heart. Flattery? An insincere compliment? No. John Wheeler, the hermit, meant what he said and said what he meant.

"An elephant's faithful one hundred percent," she giggled, quoting her favorite Dr. Seuss story.

Faithful, unpretentious, honest, she mused. The kind of man whose word was his bond. The kind of man whose handshake was his word of honor. Those were the sterling traits of an old-fashioned gentleman.

"And I'm the only female he wants to kiss," she whispered, hugging herself with glee.

Extending her arms, she twirled around in the sunshine, feeling younger than springtime. As wild and untamed as the butterfly she'd crafted. Carefree. Uninhibited by the restraints of her parents or school or work, she spun around and around until the earth spun with her. Laughter bubbled from a deep well of happiness.

She loved the feel of her hair swinging across her shoulders. For a moment, she wished she had on a full skirt with yards and yards of petticoats. She'd spin so fast she'd be able to touch them with her outstretched hands. And then, she'd stand on her tiptoes until she could grab a hunk of the blue Montana sky. Nothing could stop her.

I'm the only female he wants to kiss.

John silently marveled at her as he leaned against the building and watched her. He understood. He'd experienced the same feeling and expressed it similarly. Some called it a Rocky Mountain high: Feeling great and having to physically express it. Yes, he understood; he just couldn't believe Rebecca felt it, too.

He pushed away from the wall when Rebecca reversed her direction and started to unwind. Like a child's top, her arms tilted as her spin slowed. Her footsteps faltered. For some unknown reason, it was important for him to be there to catch her when she collapsed.

Dizzy and breathless, she felt her arms and legs and neck go limp, too limp to hold her upright. Her eyes closed, her knees sagged. She was falling—falling in love with an old-fashioned gentleman.

Expecting to collapse on the ground, she gasped when she felt strong arms wrap around her waist. Her head flopped forward, nestling against John's chest.

"Crazy," she panted, smiling. "Wonderful, but crazy."

Her eyelids were too heavy to open. Her heart beat like a wild thing. The world was still spinning, tilting askew. But she felt safe . . . safe in John Wheeler's arms. For now, that was enough, she couldn't ask for more.

John nodded as he cradled her tighter. Crazy, but wonderful. He could relate to that feeling. In fact, it accurately described his present state of mind.

He'd had the same feeling four years ago. The day his entire life had changed.

With long-legged strides he carried her past the porch of the log cabin, beyond the castle's bridge, straight to the brick wing of the house, where he kept his other treasures.

"I have something beautiful to show you," he whispered against the crown of her shiny hair. "Something no one else has seen."

Rebecca smiled lazily, eyes closed. He'd already shown her something beautiful, but it wasn't something anyone could see.

She'd found love.

"Open your eyes," John said in a hushed voice, lowering her feet to the hand-woven rug covering the slate floor in the master suite. She'd never know how much willpower he'd had to exert to keep from placing her on the white satin coverlet on his bed. He steadied her by keeping his arm around her waist. "Welcome to the private collection of J. C. Wheeler."

On shaky legs she stood facing large diamond-shaped panes of beveled lead-crystal glass. Fascinated by the vivid, irregular splashes of blue, red, and purple centered in front of each pane, she moved closer. Direct sunlight coming through from outside exploded the pure colors on the white walls and ceiling of the room. Inch by inch she was drawn forward until she was close enough to touch the uncut sapphire at eye level. Spellbound, she turned when she heard John's low laughter.

"A king's ransom," he said with pride, ambling to her side. He removed the large barrel-shaped stone from its crystal shelf and held it in the palm of his hand for her inspection. "This is the first stone I found."

Speechless with awe, Rebecca raised her eyes, silently asking for permission to touch it. John nodded. With one finger she traced a large crack imbedded deep in the sapphire.

"Colored gemstones often have inclusions. Flawlessness is rarer in sapphires than in diamonds. Unless the crack breaks through the surface, it usually doesn't affect the value of the stone."

"It's magnificent." Her admiration for John grew, knowing he'd kept the stone and positioned it in a place of honor in his collection. Its material value was unimportant to him.

John chuckled. "That spontaneous dance you performed outside reminded me of how I felt when I found it. Crazy and wonderful." He laughed aloud and shook his head. "I must have stood knee-deep in half the icy mountain streams of Montana looking for this beauty. The only thing I found was enough flakes of gold and silver to keep financing my efforts. You can imagine how crazy I felt when I found this in a bed of weathered clay."

She grinned, glad to know he had found an explanation for her foolish antics. Her dark blue eyes sparkled with love as she watched him replace the stone and choose a smaller, deep red stone.

"I found this garnet beside an anthill." He bobbed his head when he saw her skeptical glance. "Honest. I was driving down the highway daydreaming when I saw a shiny boulder that looked as if it were covered with warts."

"Warts?"

"Warts," he repeated. "I pulled off the road, jumped over a ditch, and started toward the boulder. The whole area was pockmarked with anthills, so I walked with one eye on the ground and one eye on the rock. That's when I saw this garnet. I spent the afternoon crawling around on my knees between anthills, picking up garnets, laughing like a crazy old coot. The 'warts' were garnets embedded in metamorphic rock."

"Uh-uh, J. C. Wheeler. You pulled my leg about Jennifer being your girlfriend. I'm not going to fall for the garnet-by-the-anthill story or the wart-covered-boulder story."

He dropped the stone in her hand, stood back and let his onyx eyes follow the crease down the front of her slacks. "Lovely," he commented with a sexy wink. "I'd rather stroke your leg than pull it."

"Tell me the true story about the garnet," she said, knees trembling from his compliment. John flirting with her had the same effect on her as spinning around in circles.

"I did. Garnets are unpopular with ants. They don't want them in their nests." He smiled and whimsically asked, "Or do you think they were using them for landscaping purposes?"

"I think you're crazier than I am," she retorted.

"Probably. Going crazy is an occupational risk for a prospector. What's your excuse?"

"Being with you," she quipped, returning his wink. Being with him was driving her crazy. She held the garnet up to the sunlight and pretended to appraise it. "Beautiful."

"Yes." The last consonant hissed through his lips. Her beauty rivaled his entire collection of precious stones. Her skin was smooth, flawless. Her hair shone brighter than pure gold with silver frost. Only by shoving his hands into his pockets was he able to resist claiming her.

Why resist? his frustrated libido argued. You

want her? Take her. Enjoy her, then put her on a plane and forget her.

Dammit, that's what he should have done the moment he saw her bending over the conveyor belt at the airport. He'd wanted her then. A man wasn't supposed to think about sex when he saw a lady.

In all honesty, John couldn't rationally decide how to classify Rebecca. Why wasn't she cool and aloof instead of warm and alluring? Why didn't she wear feminine dresses that hid those enticing curves of hers? Why didn't he want to put her up on a pedestal instead of wanting her in his bed? Why couldn't he decide whether she was a precious gem, or a clever synthetic?

Rebecca watched him from the corner of her eye. He'd thrust his hands in his pocket and was shaking his head. She wanted to invade his privacy by asking him what he was thinking about, but didn't.

She carefully replaced the garnet. To avoid witnessing his private war, she slowly perused the other stones. Rose quartz, amethyst, tourmaline, jasper, and petrified wood contrasted with the vibrant colors of the sapphires and amethysts. No doubt, there was a story behind each stone in his collection.

"Rebecca . . ."

Her breath caught in her throat as she turned.

His arms were open to her. The light shining in his eyes was unmistakable.

"I want to love you." His voice shook with desire. "Will you be my lover?"

CHAPTER SEVEN

Rebecca's heart sank. She shouldn't have expected a proposal, but she had. After all, John C. Wheeler was a man who'd contacted her friend Diana for one specific reason: he wanted a wife.

Uncertain of how to respond, she answered, "I'm not sure that would be a wise idea, John."

"I'm not sure it would be a good idea, either." He watched her lips thin into a straight line. Hell, he must have said something wrong, ungentlemanly. Agitated, he raked his hand through his dark hair. "Please don't misunderstand, Rebecca. I guess I jumped into the stream to pan for gold without checking to see how deep the water was." He rubbed his finger behind his ear as though it were wet.

Rebecca definitely felt as though she were in over her head. The last thing she expected was for him to agree with her. And now, she could tell he was on the verge of an apology, and she didn't want to hear one. Lord have mercy, where were those clever one-liners she'd used to hold other men at bay? The tension stringing between them was almost visible to the naked eye.

He'd intentionally set himself up for her to agree, telling him that he was wet behind the ears. She hadn't smiled or laughed or anything. He wasn't sorry he'd asked, but he began formulating an apology. "Rebecca . . ."

"Don't you dare tell me you're sorry. We're both adults, over twenty-one, unattached. It isn't unusual for a student to, uh . . ." *Rattle, rattle, rattle. She was making him increasingly uncomfortable, but she didn't know how to stop.* "Well, you know. Students often get a crush on their teacher. Don't worry about it."

Rebecca glanced at her watch to avoid looking him in the eye. Automatically, her finishing school training saved her. Posture class saved her from slumping her shoulders and skulking from his bedroom. Head erect, shoulders straight, she could have balanced a stack of books on her head as she gracefully moved across the room. Deportment class saved her from socially disgracing herself. Her polite smile was correct; her eyes stared straight ahead.

"Yes, it's getting late," she said in clipped tones. "I have several items on the agenda for today. Thank you for letting me see your private collection. The stones are exquisite."

Mother would have been proud of me, Rebecca

thought. She'd mimicked her grand exit to perfection.

Outside, she raised her head to the sky. The sun was still shining. The air still smelled of early spring blossoms. The breeze was gentle. How could that be when she felt certain her heart had been broken—cracked?

She wanted the hurt to change to anger. Inner rage could be controlled by biting her tongue. In an effort to avoid wallowing in self-pity she purposely recalled his exact words.

He'd chosen them carefully. "I want to love you," he'd said. Why didn't he stop while he'd been ahead? *I want to love you* could have meant something more than going to bed together. It could have meant: I like you and I want to learn to love you. That wasn't as pleasing to the ear as: I fell madly in love with you at first sight. But anything was better than his proposition.

He must have read the dreamy expression on her face and known she'd misinterpreted his meaning. He'd clarified any potential of future misunderstanding by adding, "I want to be your lover."

She kicked a stray pebble on the sidewalk to transfer the circle of pain around her heart to an inanimate object. Deep inside, she wished she'd been equally blunt. How would he have responded if she'd said, "I'm falling in love with you. I can't sleep with you, teach you to be a gentleman, and give you a good-luck farewell kiss before Diana matches you with another of her clients."

What had she done? She'd talked about being "wise." Had she unconsciously hoped he'd plead with her? J. C. Wheeler wasn't the type of man who pleaded for anything. He either took what he wanted or didn't want it enough to bother.

He hadn't bothered.

She kicked another pebble, harder. Thank goodness her training had come to her aid before she'd made a complete fool of herself. She sauntered off the path and headed toward the opening of the canyon. John's next lesson could wait. She needed time to absorb the lesson he'd taught her: Never let your heart overrule your head.

John laid his hand the Bronco's horn. Between blasts, he bellowed, "Rebecca!"

Jennifer had sense enough to hee-haw a reply, why hadn't Rebecca? Of course, Jennifer was also bright enough to stay in the barn where she'd be comfy and cozy. Not Rebecca.

He'd spent the last half hour running from room to room searching the house. Her clothes were there, still unpacked. She hadn't taken the Bronco. She had to be within hearing distance.

"Why doesn't she answer?" he muttered. She could have taken any of the dozen dirt roads that fanned out from the mouth of the canyon. The majority of them looped around and led nowhere. "Where the hell is she?"

Heather, dryad, and laurel bloomed, carpeting the hillsides with color. Tiny pink plants grew thick, covering the ground in "pink snow." John was oblivious to anything other than watching for movement.

He goosed the accelerator and glanced at his watch. Four hours and twenty minutes had passed since he'd stuck his foot in his mouth. "She was wise enough not to fall in love with me," he grumbled. "Why wasn't she smart enough to stay near the house?"

John considered himself practical, realistic, not prone to wild flights of fantasy. Rebecca blithely wandering out of sight of the house had activated his imagination. He'd mentally pictured her stepping into a gopher hole, breaking her leg, being unable to crawl back to him. Then he'd doubled his agony by adding a rattlesnake. Leg broken, snake-bitten, she could be sprawled beneath a bush and he'd never find her. He'd have added renegade Indians to his list of perils, but he had to draw the line somewhere.

He'd also pushed aside thoughts of Rebecca being kidnapped by the trespasser who'd ransacked his sample collection. After being shot at last night, they were probably long gone. It didn't take courage to pilfer from an empty house, but facing a twin-barreled shotgun was another matter.

"Stay calm," he ordered himself. But there was an edge of panic in his husky voice. "She may be lost, but she isn't in danger . . . yet."

He followed a winding road that eventually led to a stretch of tall trees lining Hidden Creek. A good five miles from the house, he doubted she'd walked this far, but decided to check to make certain.

Slowing the Bronco, he heard . . . he cut the engine, unable to believe his ears. He couldn't believe Rebecca had left the house in a snit, walked five miles, and was *singing* when she should have been lying on the hillside in pain.

John swung from the Bronco and charged through the underbrush like an enraged bull. "Rebecca! What the hell do you think you're doing?"

"Quick-freezing my toes?" Standing knee deep in frigid water, she grinned at the way he was flapping his arms, glaring at her. "C'mere. Look what I found."

"Out!" he roared. "Do you realize that while you've been playing in the creek, I've been going crazy searching for you?"

"Why? I'm a big girl capable of taking care of myself."

"You're a city slicker!" He pointed toward the wide, flat slab of rock near her ankle. "The last time I came here there was a rattlesnake the size of a python sunning itself on that rock."

Rebecca shrugged, unconcerned. "Why don't you stop trying to intimidate me and get over here?"

"Because you'd be safer with your hand in the rattlesnake's mouth. I'd probably drown you!"

"Temper, temper, Mr. Wheeler. Cool off. Gentlemen never raise their voices."

Her cheeky smile and her wet slacks molded against her calves and thighs wasn't helping his control. "For two cents I'd haul you out of that creek and tan your hide."

"I left my purse back at the house. Do you take credit cards?"

John's howl of frustration cut her jibe short. "You are the most aggravating, inconsiderate, sassy . . ." Her bubbling laughter ended his vilification; it demanded immediate retribution. He waded into the creek like a rank amateur rockhound.

In a matter of seconds that seemed like minutes, Rebecca saw his feet fly out from under him, his arms flailing to recover his balance, and his backside splashing into the shallow water. Blue curses exploded from his mouth.

Carefully picking her way through the submerged rocks, her mouth rounded into a small circle as she watched his shoulders emerge from the water. He shook his head. She was close enough for droplets of water to spray across her chest. She stopped, not knowing what to expect from his mercurial personality. He might cheerfully drown her, as was his original intention, or . . .

John tossed back his head, wiped the water from his face, and howled with laughter.

Inching closer, Rebecca automatically extended her hand toward him. "Are you hurt?"

"No, but I've cooled off." Ignoring her hand, he wrapped his fingers around her ankle. "You look a bit hot under the collar, Miss Sterling. You need to cool off, too?"

"Let go of my ankle, John." She giggled. She stretched her arms straight out to keep her balance as she twisted her foot to regain her freedom. "I didn't tell you to go jump in the creek."

His other hand skittered up the back of her leg, sending chills up her spine that were unrelated to the temperature of the water.

"I wouldn't be here if it weren't for you, my dear," he crooned with dangerous softness. His hand teased the back of her knee. "You're the one who likes to play around in the water while you're torturing me."

"Now, John, don't do anything we'll both regret." At any moment, she felt certain he was going to pitch her headfirst into the deeper water. His husky low voice didn't fool her. She was helpless against him. She squeezed her eyes shut, waiting for the inevitable.

Rebecca dared to open one eye when she felt both his hands climbing up the length of her legs, then closed it. She excused the audacity of his hands as they gently squeezed her buttocks, telling herself he needed the leverage to gain an upright position. His fingers spanned her waist, thumbs resting below her breasts. She wavered. Her balance was threatened, not by her loss of foothold, but by the feel of John's hard thighs as he sluggishly jackknifed against her.

Although wet from the waist down, she could only feel his body heat. His hands climbed higher, moving to her side and back. Her nipples puckered into buds when his thumbs innocently brushed against the fullness of her breasts.

My legs aren't going to be able to support both our weight. Her eyes sprang open. She wasn't supporting his weight!

Tiny droplets of water clung to his sooty eyelashes. Those onyx eyes of his danced with fun-loving light. His lips were slightly parted; enough for her to see the straight edge his teeth made.

"Enjoying yourself, Mr. Wheeler?" Rebecca asked, her tone chilly as the rivulet of water streaking down his jawline sought refuge in the cleft of his chin.

"Immensely. How about you?" His thumb brazenly skated over her nipple, then his hands settled on her hips. He nestled her in the cradle of his hips.

She could feel the solid ridge behind his zipper. Wondering if she should be thankful that she wasn't the only one aroused, she sighed, shaking her head.

"Was that a ladylike, long-suffering sigh? Or a sigh of contentment?" He swayed against her, loving her softness. Earlier she'd said "No," but right now her body was saying "Yes, yes, yes." Upstairs, in her mind, she might reject him for being a stupid clod. But downstairs, where it counted, she wanted him as badly as he wanted her.

"Just a sigh," she replied with a quiver in her voice.

Unbidden, her fingers wiped the water from his face. His hand tightened on the womanly flare of her hips, then crept lower. He massaged her. Squeezing, rubbing, coaxing her closer. Her arms had a will of their own. They circled his broad shoulders until she was on her tiptoes.

Silently she broke her vow to think with her head and not with her heart. She'd fallen for him. And, literally speaking, he'd fallen for her. Damn the consequences, full speed ahead.

She heard him suck a deep draft of air in his lungs and felt his stomach flatten. His arms tightened with rib-cracking strength. Her feet dangled in the air as he inched surefooted toward the bank of the creek.

"We're going to catch pneumonia," he warned.

Rebecca tilted her head back, her sapphire eyes glinting. "Can you think of a better excuse to spend the next week or so in bed together?"

"Lady, I don't need an excuse, but I don't want you sick." He stepped from the water and hesitated. "But I don't want to give you a chance to exercise a woman's prerogative to change her mind."

Smiling sultrily, Rebecca whispered in his ear, "We'd better get rid of our wet clothes, hmm?"

"Yes, ma'am," he readily agreed, lowering her down the length of his torso. "That blouse of yours is soaked."

Rebecca crossed her arms and reached for the ribbing at the bottom. Her breath caught in her throat as his black eyes remained on her face.

"Lady, this isn't the time to be coy."

Nor was it a time to tease, she thought, anxious to be rid of the clothing that had become cold and clammy against her skin. She shed her lessons about modesty as quickly as she shed her top. Shoulders thrown back, she welcomed the sun's bright rays.

John matched her speed. His shirt hit the gravel long before she dropped her blouse. His hands moved to the waistband of his denim jeans as she unhooked her pink lacy bra.

His eyes devoured her; her eyes devoured him.

Balanced on one foot, he tugged at the soaked denim. Sharp pebbles dug into the soles of his feet after he'd kicked off his moccasins. Jeans removed, attired only in skimpy black briefs, he watched and waited.

Rebecca fingers faltered. When she'd first seen his picture, she'd commented on his size. The snapshot hadn't done justice to his proportions. Without his beard, he no longer resembled a shaggy bear. His wide shoulders, narrow hips, and long muscular legs had a devastating effect on her manual dexterity.

J. C. Wheeler would qualify to model for a beefcake calendar, she thought, suddenly feeling inadequate.

"Need some help?"

Mutely, she shook her head, glancing down at her naked breasts.

"They're beautiful." John held out his hands. A slight tremor made his fingers shake. He hadn't the slightest idea as to why she'd paused, but he wasn't taking any chances. In three steps, he closed the gap between them. "Let me help you."

He crouched in front of her. She watched his fingers make fast work of her button and zipper. John said he'd had little contact with women, but his nimble fingers made a liar of him.

She nipped her tongue to keep her mouth from rattling. What could she say? Listen, John, I'm a city slicker, but I don't know my way around the bedroom. Bedroom? Change that to I don't know my way around the woods. Dumb. She couldn't think straight, much less talk.

She placed her hand on John's shoulder and lifted one foot when he touched her heel. Before he removed her shoe, he brushed away any sharp rocks. Hearing the sound, she glanced downward. If she couldn't stand on the creek bank, how were they going to make love?

"John?"

"Hmm?"

Her hand slid down his back as he kissed one dimpled knee, then the other. Go slow, he told himself.

"We can't do this." Her hand arched, then she pointed to rocks. "It's impossible."

Head bent, John didn't see her gesture. He remained hunkered down, but tilted his head back. His eyes slowly raised, lightly caressing her pink bikini, her tummy, the valley between her breasts, until their eyes met. What she saw in his eyes was pure agony.

She pulled his shoulders against her thighs. "I didn't mean . . . what I meant was . . ." His face nestled against her stomach as she felt his hand cup her backside. His lips began stringing rows of kisses where her waistband had left a slight mark. "Oh, John, that isn't what I meant. I wasn't going to back out at the last minute."

How could she delicately tell him that, if they tried to make love on the rocks, her lack of experience couldn't provide her with a position that wouldn't injure both of them?

"You can. I'm not the barbarian you think I am," he whispered against the sensitive flesh around her belly button.

Her fingers wove through his damp hair. "John, I want to make love with you, but . . . one of us . . . or both of us . . . are going to need first aid afterward."

He stopped kissing her, wondering what the hell she meant. Was she a virgin? At her age? It was obvious that she'd been protected and pampered by her parents, but a Swiss finishing school wasn't a nunnery. Rejecting that possibility, he could only come up with one other idea. He'd seen how she'd stared at him when he'd dropped his jeans. He couldn't hide his arousal. Compared to his size, she was a small woman, did she think he'd hurt her?

Gently stroking the back of her legs, he reassured, "I won't hurt you, Rebecca."

She was at wits' end trying to find a polite way to explain herself. Taking a deep, fortifying breath, she blurted, "We can't make love on a bed of sharp rocks!"

Rebecca felt his mouth stretch into a wide grin before she heard his chuckles.

"You won't think it's so funny when I pour

Mercurochrome on your knees," she quipped none too sweetly.

John raised to his feet and lifted Rebecca in his arms. Smiling, he gave her a smacking kiss that had nothing to do with passion, and much to do with being thoroughly delighted. His good common sense had surpassed what she'd learned in her fancy finishing school. "I've already thought of that, love."

Moments later, John gently laid her on the wide, flat rock, then went back for their clothing. He rolled her clothing inside his shirt, which made a pillow for her.

Surreptitiously, he watched her stretch like a lazy cat baking in the afternoon sun. Hot blood pumped through his lower body as she propped her head on her hand, rolled to her side, and crooked her finger toward him.

Only John would think to make a pillow for her head, she mused. His considerate gesture touched her deeply.

She rolled to her back and let the sun's rays caress her while she waited. Her mind drifted to the discovery she'd made shortly before he arrived. A lethargic smile curved her lips. She'd found something worthy of putting in his private collection. Without a doubt, this was her lucky day.

John lifted her head. Her silver-gold hair wantonly spilled through his fingers as he placed the makeshift pillow under her nape. Gold often alloys with silver, he mused silently.

In one supple movement he was beside her.

"The sky looks as though it goes on and on forever, doesn't it?" he asked, satisfied being next to her, able to look at her to his heart's content.

"Big Sky country." Small talk? Now? Only when she saw the inner fire burning in his eyes did she realize his ardor hadn't cooled. He wanted her completely relaxed and at ease with him.

"I love it here."

"Have you always lived in Montana?"

"Mostly. My dad and I roamed from hillside to mountains. Sometimes we crossed state boundaries. What about you?"

"City born. City bred."

"Parents?" He twined a lock of her hair between his forefinger and thumb. So silky, so vibrant in color, he mused, raising it to his lips.

Her eyes rounded with surprise when she saw him use the blunt cut ends of her hair to paint languorous circles along his jaw. "Two."

Tiny crows feet appeared around his eyes as he smiled at her. "Convenient. My dad was a prospector. What about your dad?"

"He keeps busy running his own company. Mom attends to the social functions."

"Do I detect a note of dissatisfaction?"

"Not if I don't have to attend. I spent my

childhood trying to get their attention by pleasing them. When that didn't work, I tried open rebellion."

His jaw tightened when he heard the loneliness in her voice. He'd been on long terms with loneliness. "Did that make them notice you?"

"Long enough for arrangements to be made to have me shipped abroad." She searched his face for pity and saw none. Her hand stole into the thick, springy mat of dark hairs on his chest. "I hated being there at first, but that changed. It was comforting to know I wasn't the only bothersome child in the world."

"I guess in that aspect I was fortunate. Mom passed away when I was little." He smiled wryly. "Mother Nature and dad raised me. Dad called me his good luck piece."

The muscles of his chest grew taut under her gentle ministrations. While they'd talked, she'd become more and more relaxed while he'd grown tense. He'd tortured himself with lambent glances, but it was sweet torture. He wouldn't have traded places with any man on earth.

Certain he'd imprinted the fragrance and texture of her hair in his mind, he uncoiled the lock he held. He traced over her facial features with his fingertips. He wanted to remember each smooth plane, each slight flaw. But she was perfect. Lovely.

Rebecca raised her hand until her fingers

touched the vulnerable, pulsating place low on his neck. His heart raced. That surprised her. He'd spoken with a deceivingly soft drawl as though he had all day to listen to her.

"Why?" she whispered, puzzled.

"Who knows? Maybe because I was his only child. He never struck gold. He had this dream of striking it rich, building a home, and—"

She pressed her fingers against his lips to still them.

"No, I meant, why are we engaging in small talk when I want . . ." She paused when he nibbled on the tips of her fingers. His breath was hot; his mouth hungry. She gathered her scattered wits long enough to whisper, ". . . when I want to kiss you."

His shoulders and head blotted the sun from the sky as he lowered his lips to hers. Sunshine haloed him as he touched her lips with his. Gently, sweetly, he molded them against hers until hers parted. Her tongue greeted his, welcoming him inside of her.

She heard his low groan, felt him shudder against her as he tasted her, letting her inner sweetness flow over his taste buds. His powerful hands framed her face. He'd held the stones from his private collection the same way—with admiration and respect. He made her feel precious, valuable. She yearned to belong to him completely.

John swirled his tongue, seeking each tiny hollow and crevice. He explored her as meticulously as if he were searching for hidden gems. With each small sound, each gentle sip, she revealed all her secrets. He discovered that when he flicked the tip of his tongue at the roof of her mouth, she dug her fingers into his shoulders. Tentative strokes along the velvet-textured center of her tongue yielded bold swirls from her. Sharp thrusts produced sibilant echoes of her heartbeat. Her secrets—he learned all of them. She gave them willingly.

Patience was a difficult lesson Mother Nature had taught him. In his youth when he'd been impatient to fulfill his dreams, he'd wandered into the hills picking up and pounding every rock he saw. In his rush he'd cover a vast amount of territory, but eventually he'd left empty-handed. Patience—taking the necessary time to learn the lay of the land—was essential.

Mother Nature also trained him to delve beneath the surface to find inner beauty. Gray limestone contained crystals of quartz, garnets, rubies, and emeralds. A rock that resembled a potato could contain a star sapphire. It took patience to find the secrets beneath the surface.

And now, he had the patience necessary to discover Rebecca's smallest secret. She was so delicate, so fragile. His fingers let the tiny golden links of her necklace lead him to the valley between her breasts. He reverently lifted the butterfly, gingerly letting it slide over her shoulder. He cupped her breast, loving how her nipple pouted, wanting more.

Rebecca waited impatiently, tempted to press her hands against the back of his head. He teased the bud with his tongue, much as he'd verbally teased her. Circling and nipping, driving her crazy. She arched against him. A sigh of pleasure passed through her lips when he took her into his mouth. It felt good. No, better than good—heavenly. His lips moved from one peak to the other until her head swam dizzily.

Low in the pit of her stomach she felt threads of passion slowly twisting, knotting, making her ache. Her legs drew upward as her thighs clamped together to quell the sensation. John stroking her legs, playing with the lace fringe of her panties as he ravished her breast by pulling her deeper inside his mouth, increased her torment. She moved restless beneath his hand, completely unaware of the slab of rock that had been weathered smooth by wind and water.

She didn't know when or how he removed the remaining piece of silky fabric between them. But a shuddering tremor ran the length of his back when she felt his hand close over the essence of her femininity. Her legs parted to give him access.

John's eyes squeezed shut as his fingers

touched her. Hot. Wet. He rubbed the hard pebble of her passion until he heard her gasp. Only then did he dare to enter her. Her hips writhed as he pressed the palm of his hand against her. He raised his head, opened his eyes, and watched the ecstasy on her face.

"Touch me," he begged, slanting one leg across hers as he raised over her. The back of her thighs rested on the front of his.

She did. At first shyly, then with wanton boldness. With his help, his scanty briefs disappeared with magical ease. Her hand curled around him.

She watched his eyes close, then slowly open, locking with hers. While he continued creating magic with one hand, he reached over her for her pillow. His fingers sought and found a small package in the front of his shirt. When she saw what it was, what he did with it, if she hadn't loved him before then, she would have fallen in love with him at that instant.

While she'd thought only of instant gratification, he'd thought of how to protect her from future consequences of their lovemaking.

"Thank you," she whispered, helping him put it on, then guiding him until she heard a hiss of air coming from his lips.

"Don't let me hurt you. I can stop. It's never too late."

With utmost care, he entered her.

She clutched his forearms; her legs wrapped

137

around his hips, pulling him deeper when he would have stopped. His eyes told her things he was unable to say. While her pliant body adjusted to him, he bent forward and kissed her with such tenderness that it brought tears to her eyes.

"Am I hurting you?" he asked, starting to withdraw.

She shook her head, too moved to speak. Tears slid from the corners of her eyes to her hairline. Taking a deep swallow, she said hoarsely, "Something of great beauty always has this effect on me."

His tongue captured a tear; he savored its salty taste, then kissed her as he filled her with splendor. He devoured her low whimpers, stoking the passionate fire burning inside of her with each thrust.

Rebecca felt herself explode from within. The blue sky filled with colors as clear and brilliant as the gems in his collection. Vibrant reds, pale lavenders, electric blues rocketed through the sky. Finally, when she felt him explode, a peaceful green cloud engulfed her.

The trill of a meadowlark singing brought her back to earth. John had moved, pulling her across his chest. With idleness her finger stroked his smooth jaw, then traced the satisfied smile on his face.

"You swooned," he said, a trifle smug.

CHAPTER EIGHT

"The French call it 'a little death,' " she replied, giving him a swift peck on the lips. She dipped her fingers into the water, then let the cool water dribble on his lips.

"I call it wonderful." He licked her fingertips. "Water never tasted so good. Liquid gold."

Rebecca grinned and reached for her slacks. "Wait until you see what I have to show you."

"There's more?" Folding his arm under his head, he chuckled. "Women have some advantages over men. You'd better wait fifteen or twenty minutes before you show me anything."

Digging into her pants pocket, she plucked a gold nugget the size of a dime and plopped it on his chest. "What do you think of that?"

"Is that what I think it is?"

"Yep," she drawled, mimicking him.

Eyes narrowing, he sat up and observed the luster of the mineral in direct light. He cupped one hand over his palm. If the sample was fool's gold or mica, it would lose most of its "shine" in the shade while the luster of gold would remain almost the same.

"Hot damn! This nugget is high grade."

"Like me?" she jibed, flinging her arms around his neck.

· John scrambled to his feet taking her with him, swinging her around in a wide circle. "What a woman!" he exclaimed, recovering sooner than he'd believed humanly possible.

Gleefully laughing, she asked, "Don't you want to know where I found it?"

"You'd tell?"

"Why not?"

"Because there might be more! This nugget alone is probably worth two, maybe three hundred dollars." His black eyes burned feverishly.

"What are you so excited about?"

"Show me a man that doesn't get excited when he has gold in his hand and I'll show you a man with copper pennies on his eyelids."

"That's ridiculous. Your private collection of gems is worth . . ."

John shook his head, unable to believe she didn't understand. "I can't believe you dawdled around with me when you could have been looking for more gold."

"Dawdled?" Miffed, she let loose of his shoulders. "From 'wonderful' to 'dawdled'?" She clamped her teeth down on her tongue to keep from really giving him a verbal lashing.

"C'mon, Rebecca. It isn't every day you strike gold, for Pete's sake!"

She bent down and scooped up her pants. Reaching into the other pocket, she pulled out a smaller nugget. "Here."

"Two! Almost the same size. You're the luckiest woman I've ever met!"

The look she shot him as she pulled on her trousers and top told him he could take her luck, the gold—and a flying leap. If he landed face down beside the rock they'd made love on, he might come up with gold fillings in his mouth!

John hastily pulled his jeans on. He knew he shouldn't ask, but he couldn't help himself. "Where'd you find them?"

"That's for me to know and you to find out." She jumped from the rock ledge to the bank without noticing the sharp rocks her foot landed on until pain ricocheted from her foot to her brain. "Ouch!"

"I don't blame you for not telling. Just because I own everything within eyesight doesn't mean you have to share."

Hands on her hips, chewing the side of her mouth to control her temper, she said in a low, lethal voice, "You keep the gold. And I'll tell you precisely where to find it." Imperiously, she pointed to the spot right under his nose.

"Is that a polite way of telling me to go to hell?" He leaped from the rock and loped to her side. "Here. Take it. It's yours! I wouldn't think of keeping it."

Rebecca stubbornly shook her head. "The rock we made love on juts into the stream. I found the nuggets there right before you arrived."

"The creek flooded last fall." Mentally he saw the configuration of the surrounding hills. "Gold is moved by water until it comes to rest wherever the velocity of the water appreciably slackens. There may be a trail of nuggets in the stream that could lead us to a major find. Wouldn't that be wonderful!"

He made an attempt to grab at her hand, but she dodged away from him. Dammit, she'd credited him with sensitivity. From the look in his eyes, making love to her came in a poor second to searching for gold. Rebecca had been second choice to both her parents. She wasn't about to place second again.

"You go ahead. I've had it. I'm going back to the house."

"C'mon, Rebecca. Come with me."

"No thanks." She tilted her nose skyward to check the tears that threatened to cascade down her cheeks. "I've had enough excitement for one day."

"You're mad."

"Me? Mad?" Furious would be more accurate.

142

She pried his fingers open and took the gold she'd found. Let him find his own gold. Shoes on her feet, she spun around to make a dash for the Bronco.

John stopped her. "Dammit, I know I'm confirming your worst suspicions. Honest. I don't mean to be acting like a clod, but I can't help it. I'm sorry."

Lips sealed, she silently peeled his fingers from her arm. "Saying you're sorry and meaning it . . ." She paused, attempting to swallow the lump lodged in her throat. ". . . means you'd never do it again. Something tells me your apology was insincere."

Knowing he'd be lying if he repeated his apology, he let his eyes plead his case. He knew he'd lost when she met them, then turned her back on him.

"Take the Bronco. I'll walk," he offered in consolation for not returning to the house with her.

He waded into the creek cursing her lack of comprehension. Even Jennifer knew the intrinsic value of finding gold. She'd patiently stood beside many a stream while he and his father had panned for gold. It wasn't as though he'd force Rebecca to get back into the water. He just wanted her with him. Was that too damned much to ask? From her reaction, you'd think he'd asked her to haul a ton of gold on her back!

Rebecca twisted the key and pressed the gas

143

pedal to the floor. The Bronco roared to life. She'd never driven a four-on-the-floor stick shift. Tears blurred her vision. One foot on the brake, the other on the clutch, she shifted the gears. The Bronco lurched forward when she accidentally popped the clutch. The engine died.

Wiping tears from her eyes, she tried again. If necessary she'd walk back to the house, to Denver, before asking a man obsessed with gold fever to help her.

She romped the clutch to the floor, changed gears, then turned the key. Determination made her grind her back molars together. She shifted back to first and eased her foot off the clutch.

"Not perfect," she muttered when the vehicle began to roll forward at less than five miles an hour, but she'd get there—eventually. She wouldn't risk having the engine stall by trying to shift into second.

She headed due west. Earlier, she'd walked in an easterly direction. Had it only been a few hours since she'd told him it wouldn't be wise for them to get involved with each other?

Her bottom lip quivered, and tears silently dripped from her cheeks to the front of her blouse. Knowing she couldn't think straight, she concentrated on driving. She wouldn't take the wrong turn and get lost.

If prizes were given for stupidity, she berated herself, she'd earned the gold in her pocket.

She pulled into the blind canyon and parked in front of the monstrosity John called home. Relieved that she'd made it, she folded her arms across the steering wheel. She gave in to the deep sobs that made her chest feel as though bands of shrinking steel threatened to cut off circulation of her life's blood.

Hurt and disillusioned, she wept until the pain eased.

She lifted her head, wiped the moisture from her face and began to make plans. Rebecca readily admitted she was vulnerable to J. C. Wheeler's peculiar brand of charm. She wasn't the kind of woman who gave herself easily without love. Deep in her heart, there was no doubt he could soothe away the hurt. She'd seldom been able to bear a grudge longer than a day or two.

There were only two choices left. Get out and get out *fast*. To stick around would be begging for disaster.

Her legs seemed weighted as she swung them from the Bronco. She didn't listen to the subtle message they were sending: you're too exhausted to move—rest—spend the night.

"No," she mumbled. "Pack your things. Leave the books behind. John has taught me far more than he's learned himself. Let him teach himself how to be a gentleman."

* * *

Three days later, John wearily trudged toward the house. Exhausted, hungry, half-sick, only the thought of Rebecca being there waiting for him gave him the energy to keep putting one foot in front of the next.

"Rebecca! Rebecca! I'm home!"

Jennifer hee-hawed and kicked the side of the barn.

"Oh Lord," he groaned. He forgotten to tell Rebecca to let Jennifer out of the barn. The poor animal was probably starving.

He glanced up at the window of the castle hoping to see Rebecca. Darkness—silent and empty darkness—was all he saw. He glanced at his watch. Noon. She must be in the log cabin fixing lunch.

"Be there in a minute, Jenny," he bellowed when the mule started braying in earnest.

He ambled to the porch, crossed it, and opened the door. "What's for lunch?"

Nothing, he answered. The kitchen was immaculate, everything in apple-pie order, but no Rebecca. Maybe she's down at the barn trying to pet Jennifer, he mused. But his optimism didn't stop the cold fingers of dread that shimmied up his spine.

Jennifer landed a solid kick against the stall door as John entered the barn. Her soulful eyes

146

accused him of neglecting her. Arching her neck, she brayed at the top of her lungs.

"Hold on to your breeches, old girl, I'm hurrying," he shouted. He scooped her regular amount of feed into a bucket. "I know you think you should pig out, but you'll make yourself sick."

He dumped the food into her feed trough. Jenny buried her nose in the food and shook her head. Pellets scattered into the hay on the floor.

John grinned. "She stuck around and fed you, didn't she?"

Snorting, Jenny continued to pulverize the pellets, refusing to look at him.

He sagged against the gate. "She's madder than get out, isn't she. I can't blame her. Hell, Jenny, it wasn't until this morning when I was washing my face that I looked down in the water and saw what I'd become. Do you know what I saw?"

He didn't expect a response. Talking to Jenny was his way of sorting through a problem. She might paw the ground, or her ears might flatten against her neck, or she might roll her eyes, but she couldn't reply.

"Dad." He rubbed the growth of bristles on his face. "Remember how I used to rant and rave at him when he heard about a fleck of gold being found? Dad would be packing up to chase his dream and I'd feel sick."

"I used to count the number of towns we

passed through during a month. Don't ask me how many. Hell's bells, I couldn't keep track of them. Dad would drive into town to pick up supplies and point to the houses and say, 'Son, I can feel it in my bones. We're going to find it. Yes, sirree, you're gonna have that house you've always wanted."

John doubled his fist. It was too late to strike out at the past; it was futile. Resigned, he sighed, then rested his head on his fingers.

"Jenny, I don't even have Dad's excuse. I have a house. More house than brains," he grunted. "Of all people, I should know the symptoms of gold fever. The old man would shuffle around when he worked part-time jobs. The minute somebody whispered, 'Gold,' I'd have to run to keep up with him. Did Rebecca show you the nuggets she found in the stream?"

He paused when Jenny lifted her head and seemed to glare at him.

"Don't look at me that way. Yeah, that's the place. I remember how you used to balk when I'd try to make you cross the creek there. I thought those stories I'd heard about m-u-l-e-s being able to sniff out gold and stand on point like a dog was bunk. Don't bat those eyelashes at me. I was wrong."

Fingers splayed, he raked his hand through his unkempt hair. He tugged at the roots as though to inflict minor punishment for his greed.

"Wrong, wrong, wrong. I had something more precious than gold in my hands. I ran off on a fool's errand and left what was valuable behind."

His hands dropped limply to his sides. "What do you think, Jenny? Am I going to wind up like Dad? Is gold fever terminal or is there some kind of vaccination I can take to prevent it? That's what scares me. Oh, Jenny girl, I don't want to live alone anymore. I don't want to talk to you to break the monotony of silence."

Sick at heart, he groaned, "Rebecca is gone, isn't she? The Bronco is gone. The house is empty. She must have fed you, then headed for the airport."

His stomach twisted into a painful knot. He'd lived off the land the past three days, but he knew it wasn't hunger that made his stomach churn.

He'd lost her.

John tasted the tears that trekked down the back of his throat. He hadn't cried since his father's burial. Never had he felt so lost and alone.

She'd really gotten to him. She was a bundle of contradictions. Soft and sweet one minute, then sassy the next. Sexy as hell and regal as a queen, he mused. Hell, he still wasn't certain whether she was a real lady or not, but he didn't give a damn. He wanted her beside him, making him laugh, making him angry, making him wonder which one of them was crazier.

He opened the stall door and walked over to

Jennifer. His hand trailed down her trimmed mane and across her back. Bending, he wrapped his arms around her neck and whispered, "What am I gonna do, Jenny? You're smarter than I am. What am I gonna do without her?"

Jennifer swished her tail, but otherwise stood perfectly still. "No answers, huh? I don't blame you for keeping quiet." He straightened and turned toward the gate. "Rebecca probably wouldn't want to marry me anyway."

Without a hee-haw of warning, Jennifer took aim and fired with her hoof.

John pivoted as he rubbed his injury. "Are you kicking me while I'm down or trying to kick some sense into my head?"

Jenny stood her ground, serenely munching her pellets.

"Dammit, I know what you thinking. You think I should crawl to Denver on my hands and knees and beg her to come back, don't you?" he bellowed. "Well, I'm not going to. A man has his pride!"

Two weeks later, John straightened his tie, ran his finger around the collar of his starched white shirt, then dropped a quarter into the pay phone and dialed.

"Feldman Enterprises. Diana Feldman speaking."

He shifted from one wing-tipped shoe to the

150

other as he cleared his throat to give the speech he'd memorized. "J. C. Wheeler. I calling in regard to one of your consultants. Rebecca Sterling. I was wondering if you could give me her phone number?"

"Mr. Wheeler, I've been expecting your call. You must be a fast learner. Rebecca says you—"

"Her number, please?" he repeated forcefully.

Diana ignored his interruption. "That you're ready for the big date. I've found your lady. A perfect match to the list you sent earlier."

"Miss Feldman, I'm not interested in your matchmaking services. I want to find Rebecca." Exasperation threaded through his voice, making it harsher than he wanted it to sound. He heard a slight gasp from the other end of the line. "I'm sorry. I didn't intend to be rude."

Diana tapped the eraser of her pencil on her desk blotter. Rebecca continued to swear that nothing had happened while she'd been in Montana, but Diana dismissed her vehement denials. Her best friend had literally gone into a decline. She wasn't eating properly. She refused to date, preferring to moon around her apartment. Oh, she claimed to be working on a rush project, but Diana knew better. Sketches would have been strewn around the tables and counter tops. Rebecca's apartment was disgustingly immaculate.

The last time Diana had mentioned J. C.

Wheeler's name, Rebecca asked, "Who?" as though she'd never heard the name. Who-hell, Diana had blasted. Ten seconds later, Rebecca had made her promise on her word of honor that she wouldn't mention his name. Should John contact the agency, Rebecca didn't want to know who he'd been fixed up with or the outcome. Should he ask about her, which Rebecca felt was extremely unlikely, Diana wasn't to give any confidential information.

"No problem, Mr. Wheeler. Now, back to your reason for contacting me. I can arrange a dinner date for tomorrow night if that's convenient."

John glared at the black receiver in his hand. Talking to Rebecca's friend was about as effective as conversing with Jennifer. "Rebecca isn't listed in the phone book. When I called the operator, I was told she has an unlisted number."

"I'm sorry, Mr. Wheeler. The agency has a company policy not to give out employees' phone numbers."

He expected that reply. "Then arrange for Rebecca to be my date tomorrow evening."

"That's impossible."

"Why?"

"I'm not at liberty to discuss Rebecca's personal life or schedule her dining arrangements." She heard his teeth grind and realized he was at the end of the tether. "Frankly, Mr. Wheeler, she put our friendship on the line."

Frustrated, not wanting to cause trouble, but desperately wanting to find Rebecca, he growled, "How is she?"

Miserable. "Fine."

"Dammit, you said that as though I'd asked you about the weather!"

Diana grinned as an idea struck her. "I can discuss the . . . uh, weather. How's *your* weather in Montana?"

Quick on the uptake, he responded, "Gloomy. Depressing." He slipped by adding, "Lonely."

"I haven't seen any rain, but cloudy skies have been on the horizon." Diana felt a twinge of guilt, but disregarded it.

"Miss Feldman, have you ever heard the riddle —what does everybody talk about, but no one does a thing about? What's that? The weather. Won't you help me do something about those clouds and the threat of rain? Please? Let me give you the number of the hotel where I'm staying. Call Rebecca. Tell her where I am. She can call or come and see me."

"How long are you staying in Denver?"

"However long it takes. One way or another, I'm going to show her I've recovered from my bout of gold fever, permanently."

Diana chuckled. "I told her that you were a man who got what he went after when I showed her your picture. The hermit and the lady. What a mismatch."

"Does that mean you'll talk to her?" he asked, smiling for the first time in weeks.

"On one condition."

"Name it."

Diana twiddled her pencil between her fingers. She couldn't demand to know if his intentions were honorable, so she put him to the test. "If Rebecca refuses to see you, you'll go out with the woman I selected."

"Unacceptable terms," he replied immediately. "Pointless. You see, Miss Feldman, I'm in love with Rebecca. I may not be the perfect gentleman, but let me assure you that I am a one-woman man."

CHAPTER NINE

Rebecca annealed the flat strip of gold with a blowtorch on a charcoal block. The metal was fairly soft. She rounded the ends by hand until they squarely, with a slight "V" channel inside, chained together. She overlapped the ends until they made a neat fit.

A labor of love, she mused, closely examining her work. Crying hadn't helped. Moping around like a zombie hadn't helped, either. Days were filled with vivid memories of sunlight and laughter; nights were filled with explicit dreams of hot kisses and sensuous touches.

To exorcise J. C. Wheeler from her mind, she'd decided to devote her mental and physical energy to crafting a piece of jewelry from the nuggets she'd found. Goldsmithing took intense concentration; it didn't allow room for flights into fantasy.

She placed a thin strip of hard solder in the V-shaped channel with a minimum amount of soldering flux to cover the joint. Then she bound the joint tightly with binding wire. With gentle heat at first, so that the flux wouldn't bubble, she dried out the moisture, and then, moving the flame of the torch about in a circular motion, she heated the joint evenly until the solder melted. Finally, she directed a sharp heat along the seam, removed the flame, and plunged her work into a pickle solution.

After rinsing it, she tapped the ring onto the mandrel with a rawhide mallet, then reversed the ring and tapped it from the other side. She'd marked the mandrel for the size of her fourth finger. Was it an accident when she struck the ring beyond the mark? No, she'd sized hundreds of rings. Rebecca shook her head and continued tapping.

As though her fingers were controlled by an impish demon, she tapped and tapped until the size of the ring was larger than her thumb. When the wide ring began to bell out a little, she held it farther down the mandrel toward the tapered end and tapped all around it with a steel planishing hammer.

She turned the mandrel upside down and watched the ring as it slid to her workbench. It made a hollow sound, hollow as the sound of her heartbeat. Her forefinger circled the inside of the ring, feeling for sharp edges.

Determined not to think about the empty feeling in the pit of her stomach, she filed away any markings, first with a coarse file and then with a fine file. She rubbed the surface all over with a Water-Of-Ayr stone to round off the sharp edges she'd felt.

Her thoughts drifted backward despite her resolve to forget about John. He was like the ring, she mused with a wry smile. Solid gold with sharp edges.

"Edges that cut," she sternly reminded herself.

With a minimum of polishing, she knew John could meet his goal of giving the appearance of being the perfect gentleman. His outside demeanor was rough, sometimes coarse, but inside she'd discovered that he was an old-fashioned gentleman—most of the time.

She mounted a tapered felt cone charged with crocus powder on a motor. After fitting the ring snugly on the cone, she flipped the switch to activate the motor. Minutes later, the inside of the ring was polished to her satisfaction. She polished the outside edge with sticks fitted with strips of leather.

Closely inspecting it, she rotated it slowly on her thumb. Smooth, she thought, silently congratulating herself. Smooth as John's cheek after he'd shaved his beard.

Rebecca blinked to erase the visual image superimposed on the glossy sheen of the gold.

Can't I work without thinking of him? she bemoaned. How long would it take to get him out of her system? A month? Six months? A year?

She rubbed the back of her hand against her forehead. "Forever?" she disparaged aloud. "What I need is a good, solid case of amnesia."

Two steps were left to finish the gold band. She needed to remove the polishes with methylated spirits and give the ring a final buffing on the motor with a soft mop and rouge compound. The surge of adrenaline that had allowed her to begin the project had dwindled to nothingness.

She didn't have the energy or the heart to finish the ring. Listlessly, she set the ring on the worktable. Feet dragging across the hardwood floor, she moved from her workroom to the living room.

Her stomach growled, but she turned a deaf ear to the low rumble. A package of crackers and an open jar of peanut butter on the cocktail table attested to her lack of appetite.

Nothing tasted good. Nothing smelled good. Nothing looked good. She'd lost her zest for living. There were moments when she wondered if she'd lost her mind as well as her heart while she'd been in Montana. She knew talking would help, but feared she'd turn into a blubbering idiot.

She slumped into the corner of the sofa.

Diana had tried to help, she recalled. They'd been friends too long for Rebecca to be able to pull the wool over her friend's eyes. Diana had probed; Rebecca had retreated behind a hard shell that was impervious.

"Maybe I need to get it off my chest," she whispered as she reached for the telephone. "Nothing else seems to work. What the hell."

She'd punched in the last number when she heard the doorbell ring. Returning the receiver to its cradle, she got to her feet and crossed to the door.

"Who's there?" she called.

"Diana."

"Great minds," she muttered, slipping the chain from the door, unlocking the dead bolt, and opening the door. "Come on in. I was in the process of calling you."

Diana's blue eyes zipped from Rebecca's lackluster hair to her bare toes. "Well, my dear, you're certainly looking chipper," she said sarcastically.

"Turn off the patter or I'll gag." Rebecca crossed to the blue and red wing chair and dropped into it. She swung one leg over its arm. "What can I do you out of?"

Diana groaned and slapped her forehead dramatically. "Cut the slang. Sit up and put your knees together, then we'll talk."

"Pajamas protect my modesty," Rebecca replied, slightly annoyed and a trifle rebellious. Diana could be damned pushy. "Take the load off your feet, kiddo."

"Terrific," Diana muttered, taking a seat on the edge of the sofa. "You've gone from being a lady in 'decline' to being bitchy. What's your next act?"

Instantly contrite, Rebecca apologized for taking her bad mood out on her friend. "I must be going stir crazy or something."

"It's the 'or something' I want to talk about. I got an interesting phone call this afternoon." Diana watched Rebecca's head snap upward. "Yeah. J. C. Wheeler called."

Rebecca grimaced. She'd known he'd call Diana eventually. He'd probably read the books she'd left behind and decided he was ready to meet the perfect lady. But she restrained from clamping her hands over her ears and refusing to listen. Perhaps if she knew he was dating another woman he'd be easier to forget.

She pushed her hair back from her face and said, "So?"

"Ahha! That's a good sign. You're curious about him."

"Okay. I admit it. I'm curious." Rebecca straightened, crossed her ankles, and twined her fingers together. Slowly her mind was coming out of its comatose state. She was feeling again. First annoyance, then curiosity. That was a good sign. Diana had pushed over across the first hurdle of

160

getting back to a normal life. "He's here. Who'd you arrange for him to meet?"

"You," Diana replied simply.

Rebecca jumped to her feet as though she'd received an electrical charge. "No."

"Why not?"

"Offhand I can think of a million reasons."

Diana noted Rebecca's agitated strides as her friend crossed the room. "Such as?"

"I don't fit the description of the woman on his list. I'm not about to put on my white underwear, ruffled blouse and calf-length black skirt for any man."

"No problem. From the sound of his voice, I don't think he cares what you wear . . . or don't wear, for that matter." Grinning, Diana added, "Next?"

"He knows me. He could have arranged a date with me while I was in Montana."

"Not when you pared your two-week assignment down to two days. You haven't told me what happened, but I surmise that you split without saying good-bye. Correct?"

Nervously pacing back and forth, Rebecca nodded her head.

"No note? No address? No phone number?"

"I marked the pages in the magazines and books I thought he should read and . . ." Diana's laughter halted her speech. "That's funny?"

"Loose ends. You've always hated them. I can

picture you, mad as hell—you were mad when you left, weren't you?"

"With good reason."

"As I was saying, mad as hell, turning the corners down on pages. You couldn't just walk out. You had to do it with style." Diana rose. "That's what's been getting to you for the past two weeks. You ran like hell, but you didn't tie up all the loose ends, did you? J. C. has some sort of emotional string wrapped around you that distance didn't snap."

Rebecca started to disclaim any emotional strings binding her, but bit her lip. What was the point in denying it?

Closing the gap between them, Diana rested her hands on her friend's shoulders. "You fell for him, didn't you?"

Mutely, Rebecca nodded her head. "Hard. I made a fool of myself—big time."

"Look at me, Rebecca." She waited until their eyes met. It wasn't her place to tell Rebecca that John loved her, too. But she could do what she did to earn a living. "Cooping yourself up behind a locked door isn't going to break the string. Snarl it, maybe, but not snap it. I know you have to be pushed to the extreme before you'll engage in open confrontation, too. I watched how your parents pushed and pulled you until you couldn't take it."

"It's not the same."

162

"Isn't it?"

Rebecca withdrew from Diana's light hold and turned to the window. There were similarities. From the beginning, neither her parents nor John wanted her. Both of them wanted a malleable "lady." In both cases, she'd tried to please them by being what they wanted, and then she'd rebelled. She'd left for Europe; she'd left for Denver. Each time she'd learned something; she'd grown. Breaking away from her parents hadn't been easy. They'd fought a major battle, but she'd won. She'd moved out of her father's home and begun her own business. She'd gained her independence.

And now? She'd lost. Lost because she'd avoided a confrontation. Lost because she'd been too scared to say "I love you." Lost because she'd been too cowardly to follow Jennifer's example by kicking him in the seat of the pants and knocking "gold fever" right out of his head.

She'd crawled into a hidey-hole to lick her wounds rather than stand up for herself.

"You're right. It is the same. I came to terms with my parents, but I didn't with John."

"He wants to see you. What are you going to do?" Diana softly asked, hoping for the right answer.

"I can run, but I'm too big to hide." Rebecca smiled. "John has my books. I think I'm going to tear a page out of his."

Diana tilted her head, perplexed.

"The page entitled, *Grab for Your Goal.*" She marched toward her bedroom with Diana trailing close on her heels. "Did he tell you where he can be reached?"

"His phone number is in my purse."

"Good. Call him. Tell him to be here at eight this evening. Sharp."

Giggling at the light of battle shining in Rebecca's eyes, she said, "You're gonna give him hell, aren't you?"

"I'm going to give him everything he asks for —plus some. Then, he's going to think my ancestors were crawdads. I'm going to grab him and hold until lightning strikes both of us!"

"That's the spirit. Is there anything else I can do to help?" Diana asked.

Wheeling around, Rebecca rushed across the room and gave her best friend a hug. "Call your favorite caterer, order something elegant, and have it delivered here shortly before eight. I'm starved, so get something filling."

"Done. Italiano, not French."

A wicked gleam lit Rebecca's sapphire eyes. "Mile-long spaghetti would be marvelous—with lots of sauce."

"Hold the garlic bread?"

Grinning, Rebecca answered, "Yeah. But don't forget dessert."

"Gotcha!"

"Those were the exact words John used for a sneak attack from behind."

Laughing, Diana headed back into the living room. "With the food attacking from behind and you outflanking him, he doesn't have much of a chance, does he?"

"Don't underestimate J. C. Wheeler. He isn't going to arrive unarmed."

Rebecca searched through her wardrobe looking for the right outfit. She could hear Diana placing calls in the other room. "Careful what you tell him," she warned when she overheard John's name spoken.

"Yes, she's agreed to have dinner with you."

John's heart skipped a beat. "Where? When? What time?"

"Her place."

"Just a minute." He pulled a piece of stationery and a pen from the nightstand beside the bed. Listening carefully, he wrote Rebecca's address. Hand shaking, his handwriting resembled a child's scribbling. He repeated it to make certain he had it.

"Eight o'clock. Sharp."

"I'll be there." Resolved to putting his best foot forward, he lowered his voice and said, "One of the books said a gentleman brings flowers. What kind is her favorite?"

"Red roses."

He racked his memory to think of anything else the book recommended. "Wine? A dinner guest is supposed to bring wine, isn't he?"

Diana chuckled, tickled by the eager tone in his voice. "Red wine."

"Anything else? Cloth napkins? She's a real stickler for napkins." John suspected Diana was calling from Rebecca's apartment. He hoped Diana would ask Rebecca, then at least he'd have the sound of her voice to fortify him for the next few hours.

"She's responsible for the table settings."

"Hmm. Mrs. Feldman?"

"Diana," she corrected. "Since you're dating my best friend formalities aren't necessary."

"You'll get your bonus check, one way or the other," he promised.

"Thanks, John. I'm beginning to see why . . ." Diana stopped before she said too much.

"Yes?"

Diana substituted, "I'm beginning to see why Rebecca says you're a smart man," for her original thought, which was, "I'm beginning to see why Rebecca fell for you."

John winced as he remembered the little white lie he'd told. To cover his insecurity, he chuckled, saying, "Sometimes it takes a good swift kick to get me headed in the right direction."

"Good luck, John. I'll be rooting for you. 'Bye."

John put the receiver down. "Yeah. Good luck. I'm going to need it."

Clapping her hands, Diana bound from the sofa. "It's all arranged. He'll be here at . . ." Her mouth dropped as she entered the bedroom and saw the dress Rebecca had chosen. "You're not wearing *that,* are you?"

"You don't like the color?" Rebecca asked sweetly.

"White is fine, but . . ."

"Shush. Believe me, I know what I'm doing."

"But . . ." Diana sputtered.

" 'Bye, Diana," Rebecca said cheerfully. "Thanks for everything."

"Bite your tongue! That wasn't a subtle way of telling me to leave. Frankly, my dear, I think I'd better stick around and give a clothing consultation." She pointed to the dress, shaking her finger. "You're going to be stubborn about this, aren't you?"

"Yep." Her mouth stretched into a cheeky smile that felt great. "Trust me. I know what I'm doing."

"Hmph! My ex-stockbroker said the same thing right before the stock he picked plunged to an all-time low and my cash flow came to a screeching halt."

Rebecca waved. " 'Bye, friend. I'll call you tomorrow."

"You're taking a helluva chance," Diana said in a final warning.

"It'll be worth the risk."

Diana turned to leave. "My ex-stockbroker said that, too."

"Everything worked out. The stock did rise. Why'd you fire him?"

Giggling, Diana moved faster. "I don't mix business and pleasure, if you know what I mean." She paused at the door. "Uh, Rebecca, don't call too early in the morning. Okay?"

Rebecca caught her friend's hidden meaning and flashed her a wink. She didn't plan on getting out of bed early, either.

CHAPTER TEN

At the stroke of eight, John pushed Rebecca's doorbell button. Nervously, he fiddled with the cummerbund at his waist and polished the tip of his shoe on the backside of the opposite trouser leg. "Dressing like a hoity-toity gentleman isn't what it's cracked up to be," he muttered.

On the other side of the door Rebecca gave her apartment one final inspection, took a deep breath to steady her nerves, and reached for the doorknob. To achieve the effect she wanted, Rebecca opened the door in slow motion.

She'd practiced a hundred different ways to say "Come in", but seeing John framed in the door robbed her of all of them. Her heart kicked into double time; her tongue stuck to the roof of her mouth.

During the years she'd spent in Europe, she'd seen a multitude of men dressed in a black tuxedo with black satin lapels, but none of them filled their tux the way John did. He'd had his dark hair trimmed and shaped; it barely touched the back of his collar. The stark whiteness of his pleated shirt accentuated his tanned complexion. Without touching his jaw, she knew how it would feel: smooth.

Mutely, she gestured for him to come in.

John stood in the threshold feeling like a Montana boulder, with no mouth, no feet, and no legs to carry him inside. He fiddled with the bouquet of long-stemmed red roses in his hand to hide the unsettling rage of desire he was experiencing.

She'd worn her hair up with sexy little curls dangling beside her ears. It was the kind of hairdo that made a man want to remove the pins and watch the silky swaths cascade down from their high perch on the crown of her head. Sweet, but sassy, John mused.

His eyes avoided hers and dropped to her dress. He couldn't recall the name of the fabric—satin? taffeta?—but it made him want to slide his fingers across the slippery surface. The neckline was demure. Chaste. He hated it. Capped sleeves poofed out as though filled with air. The skirt was full—barely reaching her knees—and also poofed out. He couldn't help but wonder what she was wearing underneath to make it stand out.

Lord have mercy, he didn't dare think about what was under her feminine frippery. He'd start howling like a coyote in love!

Rebecca recovered before John did.

"Come in, please," she said graciously. A genuine smile curved her pink lips when she saw how he'd mangled the green tissue paper surrounding the flower stems. "Are these for me?"

Her soft, seductive voice jarred his tongue loose. "Only if you take the vase holding them," he quipped, his sense of humor saving him.

Chuckling, Rebecca took the flowers and responded, "You don't look like a man who'd be comfortable perched on the top shelf of a cabinet after the blossoms wilt."

"I'm not." He relinquished the bottle of Chianti along with the flowers.

"Then I'd better put these in another vase, hadn't I?"

When she turned toward the kitchen, she heard John inhale. She knew why. From the front her dress was almost puritanical: white, high-necked, full-skirted. Very, very ladylike. The back, what there was of it, was entirely different. A deep vee plunged from shoulder to waist. A saucy fluff of net created the illusion of an old-fashioned bustle, but she knew it called attention to her small waist. Intentionally she let her hips sway provocatively as she left the room.

"Would you like something . . . to drink?"

"White lightning." If dresses were given names, that's what he'd have called hers. Small beads of perspiration dotted his upper lip. There wasn't a muscle in his body that wasn't tense. "On the rocks. A double."

"Will gin do? Moonshine isn't sold in city liquor stores," she called from the other room.

"Ice water, then, please."

John removed the handkerchief from his pocket and dabbed his mouth.

"Why don't you take off your coat and tie and make yourself at home?" she suggested.

Self-preservation motivated her offer. Looking at him the entire evening while he was dressed to kill was beyond endurance. She'd thought him handsome in faded jeans and flannel shirts. In a tux he was utterly devastating.

"Are you certain you don't want something stronger than ice water?"

"No thanks." Grateful to be rid of at least part of his monkey suit, John did as she instructed. He removed the cummerbund also. Mentally he recited his lessons on what to do and not do to keep his mind from wandering back to exactly what she was or wasn't wearing under that dress.

"Please, sit down," she said after she'd given him his water and put the roses in the center of the cocktail table. "How's Jennifer?"

He waited for her to sit down, then sank on the white leather sofa. "Fine. Ornery as ever."

"Who feeds her when you're gone?" she inquired, remembering how guilty she'd felt about deserting Jennifer without knowing how long John would be gone or how much to feed her.

"I let her loose." John sipped his water, then placed it on the glass end table. He noticed Rebecca's hands were empty, folded primly on her lap. "She lives off the land."

"Oh."

John's eyes focused on her rounded lips. Hers were soft and inviting; his were parched. He licked his, wishing he could do the same to hers. "Thanks for putting the hay in her stall."

"It never occurred to me to let her roam free."

It also never occurred to her to keep her eyes from roaming freely over John. Her social graces were sadly remiss and she was running out of small talk, fast.

Their eyes met, skittered away in opposite directions, and then were drawn back until they held.

She'd seen his dark eyes glow like that twice. Once, when they were making love, and second, when he'd seen the gold she'd found. Gold fever. She lowered her lashes to hide a momentary flash of pain.

"She socked it to me when I returned. I deserved it." John leaned forward and covered Rebecca's hand. "Didn't I?"

Rebecca worried her bottom lip. This wasn't going how she'd planned. She hadn't expected open confrontation this early in the evening. She should have known John wouldn't beat around the bush indefinitely.

"Yes," she replied with blunt honesty. She couldn't allow herself to graciously excuse his behavior. He had deserved a good swift kick where it would do the most good. But he was rushing her; he could feel it.

"Any more problems with the trespasser?"

"None." Withdrawing his hand, he added, "Must have been a drifter who thought the house was temporarily abandoned. You know how wary I was of strangers." He saw her nod. "The week prior to your arrival, I was in a canyon. Out of nowhere from overhead rocks started pelting the Bronco. Combining that information with the shadows moving around that I saw the first night you were there made me overly anxious."

"Aren't you worried now?"

John swiped his hands across each knee, shot her an engaging smile and answered, "Yeah. I sure am. But not about someone breaking into the house."

As far as Rebecca was concerned, he had little to worry about on that score. One more heart-wrenching smile and she'd be on his lap pronto. No, she silently scolded. Settle your differences first.

From the tightening of her mouth, John assumed he'd crossed into dangerous territory.

He'd have to be patient. "Dinner smells great. Can I help you serve it?"

His unexpected change of topic flustered her. She'd bolstered her courage to begin the head-to-head conflict and he'd changed tactics, knocking her mentally off balance.

"Everything is ready." She popped out of the chair; her crinolines swished sassily. "I should have realized eight o'clock was past your normal dinner time."

John grinned. Now he was getting somewhere. She'd been altogether too calm and cool for his liking. He quickly moved to the table and pulled out her chair, then he seated himself across from her where another setting of silver had been placed.

"I read the pages you marked and I'm ready for my first big test," he teased lightly. He removed the napkin with his left hand, gently shook the folds loose, and draped it over his lap. "One napkin in the lap, not tucked under the chin."

"Well done," she complimented with saccharine sweetness. She could have cared less if he'd tied it around his neck; table manners were the least of her concerns. "Help yourself to salad dressing while I serve the entrée."

John shook his head. The wine had to be opened, sampled, and poured first. He undid the cork. "I should let it breathe, shouldn't I?"

"Chianti is robust. Go ahead and pour it."

She was having too much trouble with her own breathing to be bothered with whether or not the wine got enough oxygen. His long legs were close enough to her silk stocking clad ones for her to feel his body heat.

Tucking her legs beneath her chair, she avoided temptation. She lifted the lid on the silver chafing dish and served him a hearty helping of spaghetti. Let's see you get your mouth around those, she silently challenged.

After he passed Rebecca the salad dressing, he waited for her to pick up her fork and take the first bite. That was his cue. From then on, all he had to do was copy whatever she did.

Deftly, she singled out two strands with her fork and twirled them on a large spoon. He watched the small bite disappear between her lips. That couldn't be too tough.

John picked up the correct silverware and copied what she'd done. A look of dismay crossed his face when the amount of spaghetti on his fork kept growing larger and larger. There was no way he could get his mouth open wide enough to accommodate it. He shook the noodles off and tried again. He twisted and twisted until there appeared to be more wrapped around his fork than was left on his plate.

"Did you make the dressing?" he asked politely, putting his fork on his plate and picking up the salad fork.

"No. Diana called a catering service for me."

"Guess that's one advantage of living in the big city, huh?"

"I wouldn't know," she replied truthfully. "I enjoy cooking. It's one of those things I wasn't allowed to do while I lived at home."

John wiped his lips. He could have given her a big smacking kiss for letting him know she wasn't dependent on the local caterer. In some small way was she telling him she wouldn't mind the isolation of living with him in Montana? His hopes soared.

He raised his glass, silently toasting her, then sipped his wine. His mouth puckered. It was awful. Expensive, but unpalatable, he thought as he set it aside.

From the corner of his eye, he watched Rebecca twirl another bite of spaghetti. How could something look so simple and be so difficult? Determined to match her skill he tried again and failed.

"Everything is delicious," he commented.

Rebecca felt a twinge of guilt as she swallowed. She'd expected revenge to be sweet; it wasn't. "There's a knack to eating spaghetti. When it seems like it's a mile long, you start out with two noodles."

177

"Thanks. The polite way to eat spaghetti wasn't on one of the pages you marked."

"The loose ends will dribble sauce on your shirt. Be careful," she warned. She put her fork on the plate and watched him. "Speaking of loose ends, I invited you to dinner to tie up some loose ends I left dangling by running back to Denver."

John successfully managed to get a bite in his mouth without mishap. After he chewed and swallowed, he said, "I'm not certain we should discuss this at dinner."

"Why?"

"The books says serious discussions are saved for after dinner. Besides, I don't think what you want to talk about can be adequately discussed at the table. The book says . . ."

"To discuss items of mutual interest," she quoted. "That's what we're going to do."

"Isn't talking about s-e-x during dinner worse than mentioning celibacy at the breakfast table?" he goaded.

She glanced at him and saw a devilish gleam in his black eyes. "We aren't going to discuss sex."

"Oh." He looked upward as though mentally leafing through the pages she'd marked to find what page she was on. "Now I remember. We're on the chapter that deals with being tactful—telling each other polite little lies. Ladies first," he obliged. "Why didn't you stick around and enjoy my hospitality?"

Rebecca tossed her napkin on the table as though flinging down a white glove. "Hospitality?" She gasped.

"Now, now, be tactful," he jibed. "I generously offered you the use of my Bronco and you indicated you were going back to the house. I don't recall your telling me how much you enjoyed staying with me and then offering to reciprocate by letting me enjoy your hospitality."

Scooting her chair back, Rebecca said, "Excuse me!"

"You're excused," John replied blandly. He covered his smile with his napkin as he watched her flounce from the room. "Does your leaving the table mean we've finished dinner? No dessert?"

"Yes," she hissed. "As far as I'm concerned we're finished."

John stood and crossed to the living room. "We aren't finished. We've only just begun."

"All right! Let's begin. Forget about the etiquette book. Off with the white kid gloves and down to brass knuckles."

"Suits me, love," he agreed amiably.

"Speaking of suits, I thought when you arrived wearing a *tuxedo,* and bringing me roses that you sincerely regretted making love to me and then running off into the hills," she jabbed.

"Now we're getting somewhere." He leaned against the doorjamb, loving her fire, her spirit.

He wanted to draw closer and warm himself, but he shoved his hands in his pockets instead. "That was crass and I humbly apologize."

Knowing he never apologized without meaning it made her feel as though she'd taken a swing at an unarmed man. It completely shattered her attack. "Dammit," she murmured, "you're fighting dirty."

"But I am sorry," he repeated. "I owe you an apology and an explanation. Of all people, I should have had a natural immunity to gold fever. My dad had it. I know what it did to him. It turned both of us into rootless vagabonds. Rest assured that I won't let that happen to me and my family. I had a touch of the fever, but it won't reoccur. You cured me."

"I did?"

"I'm burning up right now, but it isn't from gold fever. I want you, Rebecca Sterling."

She ducked her head, unable to bear looking at his flaming eyes. "You really do know how to fight dirty, don't you?" she mumbled.

"Yeah, I do." He straightened and slowly walked toward her. She might as well hear the worst part, he decided. "I told you a lie that wasn't a white one. It was a bold, black lie to cover something I've always been ashamed to tell." He stopped a foot away from her. "I didn't graduate from college. Hell, I didn't graduate

180

from high school. Mother Nature was my mama and a hard life was father."

Automatically, she reached to cover his lips. His eyes brimmed with flicker of pain. He caught her hand, shaking his head.

"That only makes me ignorant, not stupid. Save your pity for someone who needs it." He brushed his lips across her knuckles. Telling her the whole truth wasn't as painful as he'd anticipated. "Oh, I know a lady is supposed to be sympathetic, but I learned a couple of things while I was reading those pages you marked . . . and the ones you didn't mark."

"What?" she whispered.

"First of all, my idea of what made a woman a real lady was as shallow as the creek where you found the gold. How a woman dresses and smells and pretends to act doesn't have anything to do with being a *real* lady. Not any more than those same things have to do with being a gentleman."

Rebecca smiled. "I knew you were a gentleman almost immediately."

"Let me finish," he warned. "Did you think about why you marked certain pages and not others?"

"Certainly. Some things are important and others aren't."

"Uh-uh. The pages you marked were the things a boy learns to avoid making grave social blunders on his way to becoming a man. I read

181

some of the other pages to Jennifer and she agreed with me. With her hee-hawing she expressed her sentiments and mine."

"Some of the authors did go to the extreme," Rebecca admitted. She wasn't going to waste her energy defending petty, meaningless rules. John was taking the long way around to get to his point, but she knew she was still in for some surprises. There was a time to fight and a time to duck. Rebecca ducked his verbal swing.

John nodded and threw another punch—directed only at himself. "You came to Montana expecting to find a barbarian and you did. And you knew I was a hermit. What you didn't know is why I chose to live alone."

"Because you don't like people?" she parried.

He tightened the grip on her hand. "Wrong. I wasn't protecting myself from others, I was protecting them from me. And me from myself," he tacked on truthfully. "I learned at an early age that I wasn't the kid that was going to be invited into a boy's home to share dinner. And the girls' mothers weren't going to let me skip rope with them, either. My manners were atrocious. I wanted to do the right thing, but I hadn't the vaguest notion of what the right thing was."

"That wasn't your fault," she protested, coming to his defense.

In a flash, she realized what she should have known all along. John loved her enough to let her see him through his own eyes. He wasn't going to hold back any punches, but they were all aimed at Jennifer's favorite target.

Once he'd started, he couldn't stop. "I have more flaws than a worthless gem, so rather than let anyone closely examine me, I hid out in the rocks. There's one problem with encasing oneself in granite. It's damned lonely. That's when I decided to do whatever it took to find myself a lady."

He laughed at himself. "Strike it rich, build a home, and marry a fine lady. Dad's dream. Until you came into the picture, I'd made it my own. You shattered my illusion from the moment I saw you bending over to save your precious box of china. To be honest, I thought it was pure lust, which caused a problem. I thought a man only lusted after a woman. A man never lusted after a lady. I tried my damnedest to put you up on a pedestal, but you kept your feet firmly planted on the ground."

Rebecca uncurled his fingers as he spoke and brought his palm to the side of her face. "A woman can be a lady—and a lady can be a woman."

"Of all the things you tried to teach me, that was the hardest lesson to learn. The second hardest lesson I learned was to accept myself for what I am. I'll never be without flaws. I can polish and polish until I look like a fancy stone, but deep inside those old insecurities will still be there. I am what I am."

He reached into his pocket and pulled out a stone Rebecca hadn't seen in his private collection. "It's the first star sapphire I found," he said, his voice hoarse with emotion. He'd taken chances with his life before by entering deserted mine shafts and caves, but never had he felt as though he were taking his life and putting it in someone else's hands. "I want you to have it because I want you to be the lady in my life. I love you, Rebecca Sterling. Do you think you could take this stone and make a special wedding ring?"

Rebecca opened her hand and took the stone. Tears filled her eyes, which made the six-sided star seem to wink at her. Speechless with delight, she grabbed him around the neck and gave him a big kiss.

"Does that mean yes? You'll marry me?" he asked, swinging her around in his arms.

"Yes! Yes! Yes!" Each *yes* was punctuated with a string of loud kisses. "But on one condition."

"Yes. Whatever the condition is I'll agree to it," he promptly responded.

She squirmed from his tight hold, took his hand, and led him into the bedroom. Raising one dainty hand, she gestured toward the bed. "You have to wear what's tucked under the pillow."

As he crossed the width of the room, Rebecca reached for the single hook-and-eye at the back of her waist. She watched his hand disappear, and hoped the golden ring would fit. Once he put it on, she never wanted him to take it off.

"It's beautiful. You made it from the first nugget you found, didn't you?"

Rebecca nodded, proud of the ring, proud of him, and proud of herself. "Read the engraving on the inside."

He held the ring close and silently read it. He closed his eyes and asked, "Ever seen a mountain man cry?"

"All my love to J.C.W.—the perfect gentleman." The tiny engraved words had come from her heart. She unhooked her dress and let the bodice fall. The stiff crinoline petticoats kept it from sliding to the floor. "I have imperfections, too. You don't see mine and I can't see yours."

John's onyx eyes flamed. He slipped the ring on his finger. It fit perfectly. He reached for her, letting the gold catch the light. "I want to love you."

She'd heard those same words before, but she hadn't known their meaning then. "I'm certain that's a wise thing to do," she replied.

John wrapped her in his arms and kissed her with a passion that burned brighter than the gold she'd found. Within moments they were both on fire. Her plans of slowly removing each petticoat went up in smoke.

Within magical moments they were locked in

an embrace that was as intimate as it was fulfilling. John claimed her; Rebecca claimed him. Together they staked claim on a love more valuable than his private collection.

Afterward, John held her close in his arms while she rained delicate kisses on his face. "Your brow is feverish," she said huskily. "Should I be worried?"

John gave her a lazy wink. "Believe me, I'm not going anywhere."

She did. Returning his wink, she boldly ran her hand from his shoulder to his thigh and said, "The only gold you're going to chase is a golden anniversary. Right?"

Grinning, John nodded his head. "C'mere, lady. I think we'll practice that last lesson over and over until I get it perfect."